Totall

Darker
Darkest

Sure Mastery
Unsure
Sure Thing
Surefire

The Hardest Word
A Hard Bargain
Hard Lessons
Hard Choices

A Richness of Swallows
Rich Tapestry
Rich Pickings

What's her Secret?
The Three Rs

Collections
Paramour: Re-Awakening
Jolly Rogered: Right of Salvage

A Richness of Swallows

RICH PICKINGS

ASHE BARKER

Rich Pickings
ISBN # 978-1-78430-239-9
©Copyright Ashe Barker 2014
Cover Art by Posh Gosh ©Copyright September 2014
Interior text design by Claire Siemaszkiewicz
Totally Bound Publishing

This is a work of fiction. All characters, places and events are from the author's imagination and should not be confused with fact. Any resemblance to persons, living or dead, events or places is purely coincidental.

All rights reserved. No part of this publication may be reproduced in any material form, whether by printing, photocopying, scanning or otherwise without the written permission of the publisher, Totally Bound Publishing.

Applications should be addressed in the first instance, in writing, to Totally Bound Publishing. Unauthorised or restricted acts in relation to this publication may result in civil proceedings and/or criminal prosecution.

The author and illustrator have asserted their respective rights under the Copyright Designs and Patents Acts 1988 (as amended) to be identified as the author of this book and illustrator of the artwork.

Published in 2014 by Totally Bound Publishing, Newland House, The Point, Weaver Road, Lincoln, LN6 3QN, United Kingdom.

No part of this book may be reproduced, scanned, or distributed in any printed or electronic form without permission. Please do not participate in or encourage piracy of copyrighted materials in violation of the authors' rights. Purchase only authorised copies.

Totally Bound Publishing is an imprint of Total-E-Ntwined Limited.

If you purchased this book without a cover you should be aware that this book is stolen property. It was reported as "unsold and destroyed" to the publisher and neither the author nor the publisher has received any payment for this "stripped book".

RICH PICKINGS

Dedication

This book is dedicated to Hannah and John, as ever, with grateful thanks for their continued patience.

Chapter One

I go back into Dan's bathroom to clean my teeth and emerge to find the bedroom empty. Unless you count his elegant morning suit hanging on the front of his wardrobe, that is, looking very *Downton Abbey*. I stroll over to it, fingering the sleeve of the long-tailed dark gray jacket. Fine cloth, expensive. I wonder if he hired it, or it's his own suit. Apart from weddings, there can't be much call for this sort of thing. The waistcoat, in a lighter gray, hangs inside the jacket, making a striking contrast. The trousers and Dan's pale blue tie are draped haphazardly across the bed. I instinctively straighten and smooth them, jumping back guiltily as the door opens.

Dan comes in, a tray balanced precariously on one hand and his pristine white shirt hanging from the other. He back-heels the door closed again before depositing the tray on the bedside table. He lays the shirt on top of the trousers, glancing curiously at me as he does so. He probably knows I've been moving his things. Just wait until he sees what I just did to his bathroom, not only his toothbrush and shaving gear lined up perfectly, but now all his other toiletries arranged in order of size. It's a bad habit, I know that. But I can't seem to help myself. I contemplate nipping back in there to mess things up again but the delicious aroma of toast and bacon assaults my nostrils, and my stomach grumbles noisily. Dan's smile is wry as I peer eagerly at the tray.

"I knew you'd be hungry. I went down for my shirt and found my little brother on breakfast duty so I relieved him of some supplies. I don't want you fading away from hunger—I have plans for you. I wasn't sure what you'd like, but we've got toast, bacon, some scrambled eggs, even a few mushrooms I found in the bottom of the oven. I think he was saving those for himself, but life's a bitch sometimes. Help yourself. Oh, and there's coffee. Lots of coffee. Are you done in there? I still need to shave." He heads for the bathroom. So much for trashing it again before he sees it.

In any case, my mouth is watering. This is like being back at Freya's—she was always bringing me food in the hope of fattening me up. It's never worked, but I've no objection to folk trying.

"Thank you. I'm starving. Shall I share it out?" It doesn't seem as though he intends to eat with me, but it's only polite to offer. I'm working on my manners.

"I've had mine. I ate at Tom's before I came back over here. That's all for you. Barney followed me up here so I daresay he'll help you out with any leftovers."

I perch on the side of the bed, and pick up a rasher of bacon. I take a bite and chew happily. Dan's brought me very generous portions, but my stomach feels as though my throat's been cut and I doubt there'll be much left over for this Barney character.

"Who's Barney? Another friend of Tom's?" I reach for a fork to shovel up some of the egg.

Dan stops, turns, heads back for the door to the landing. "You must remember Barney. You met him yesterday." He opens the door and leans out. "Barney! Come on in and say good morning to Summer. You might even part her from a slice of bacon if you look sharp about it." He glances back at me as a second rasher disappears down my throat. "Or perhaps not..."

I stand, startled. I'm wrapped in just a bath towel, in no state to make polite conversation with new friends. Dan stands back to allow the newcomer in, and I gasp as the dog, which masquerades as a mountain lion, strolls calmly into the room and plonks itself down at Dan's feet.

I recall seeing him yesterday as I arrived, just before Dan's unexpected appearance sent every coherent thought from my head. And yes, Rosie did say the massive dog was called Barney. He and Rosie headed off for a walk, then he spent the rest of the evening in her bedroom while the party was going on.

"Idiot mutt. She's the one with the bacon, not me." Dan nudges the great hairy monster with his toe as I stare at it.

Up close this...creature is what my gran would have described as built like a brick shit-house. He's huge. Absolutely fucking gigantic. Dark brown mainly, with some black here and there, his fur is thick and long. His dark brown eyes are gentle enough I suppose, which is certainly a welcome feature. But the sheer size of him is overwhelming. His shoulder comes to waist height on Dan, and I swear the floor shakes as he moves. I can only stare. He seems a lot bigger in here than he did when we were outside on the front steps.

"What. Is. That?"

"That's Barney. He likes bacon."

"Is he a dog?" I have my doubts. "Does he eat whole pigs?"

"Yes, he's a dog. A Newfoundland or maybe St Bernard, with some Great Dane thrown in I reckon. And no, no pigs. He's civilized. And friendly." As if to prove the point Dan crouches to sink his hands into the thick ruff of fur around the dog's neck, rubbing vigorously.

The behemoth responds by rolling onto his back, his massive paws in the air and kicking wildly as Dan rubs his huge chest. I have to admit, Barney doesn't look dangerous exactly. Even so, I'm unnerved.

Dan stands, and the dog does too. He seems to notice me at last and ambles over to sit in front of me."

"He likes to have his ears tickled. Like you do."

"Even so, if you want me to roll on my back with my legs in the air, you have only to ask."

"How obliging of you, Miss Jones. I'll remember that. Now, can I leave you two to get acquainted or would you prefer me to shove Barney outside again?"

I'm on the point of asking him to do just that, when Barney takes matters into his own hands. Or would that be paws? He lays his head on the bed, gazing up at me, his expression one that I could only describe as pleading. I'm not daft. I know it's the bacon that he's taken a shine to, not me, but I haven't the heart to have him evicted.

"No, he can stay. I like dogs. It's just, well, he was a bit of a shock." I reach out tentatively to pat the huge head.

Barney closes his eyes, his massive tail wagging slowly.

"Good dog. Good Barney." *I hope.*

"Don't let him on the bed. Or near my suit. I don't want to be brushing hairs off my trousers all day." With a final, dazzling smile Dan disappears into the bathroom, leaving me to share my breakfast with a furball the size of a small planet.

Barney and I make short work of the food. He could throw his weight about but he's a very well-mannered, patient dog, waiting for me to pass him his share. I find myself ruffling the fur on the top of his huge head, which he seems to like. His tail thumps the floor in a slow, contented rhythm. I'm not sure if he's allowed to lick the plate but decide to let him. I daresay it'll go in the industrial sized dishwasher down in the kitchen so hygiene won't be compromised.

"Right you. You might be able to loll around eating bacon all day but I've a wedding to get to." I remember Dan's admonition regarding his suit and decide it might be best to encourage Barney to wait elsewhere while I finish getting ready. Luckily he's a biddable type and I have no difficulty shoving him back out into the corridor. I expect he knows the food is all gone so he may have been about to take his leave in any case. I shut the door on Barney and head for Dan's bathroom to join him. I need to rinse my hands.

* * * *

The wedding is fabulous. Low-key, under-stated, but simply beautiful. Tom, Dan and Nathan are quite splendid in expertly fitted morning suits. Nathan is the best man and Tom has ushering duties so I traveled over to Greystones with Eva, Rosie and baby Isabella. Dan's kiss in the bedroom as Nathan hollered up the stairs at him to get his arse in gear delivered plenty of promise for later, and my pussy is clenching and moistening in gleeful anticipation as I try to pay attention to the serious proceedings we're gathered to witness.

The wedding passes in something of a blur, my mind firmly fixed on a point somewhere a little later in the day. I sit, stand, sing and pretend to listen as the registrar leads us through the service. I'm aware that the vows have been exchanged, the bride-kissing executed with a degree of enthusiasm which I'd describe as bordering on raucous, but maybe that's just me.

The formalities concluded, I follow the rest of the party outside to the marquee where the food is being served, to nibble on dainty little sandwiches. Or maybe they're canapés. I'm really not paying attention, my head is somewhere else entirely. And my pussy is bent on betrayal, moist and hot, spasming hard at the most inopportune moments.

"Sparkling wine, Summer?"

"Yes, thank you…" *Spasm.*

"Would you like a slice of wedding cake?"

"No, I already…" *Clench.*

I'm nervous, excited, disgustingly wet, and having the time of my life.

The music is lively, much of it delivered by Rosie and Eva. Not much of a dancer myself, I spend much of the afternoon chatting with Freya, and Eva when she's not playing her violin. I'm acutely conscious of Dan's presence as he moves around the guests. He occasionally catches my eye, a swift smile, a brief wink the only signals that there's more between us. It's enough though, and I'm happy to let the day float past me in a pleasant haze.

Freya and Eva seem to have become firm friends and I listen quietly while they discuss Tom's latest business project, a proposed wind farm. Freya is very interested in the details, and even if she hadn't already told me her intentions, I'd recognize the signs. I resolve to find an opportunity as soon as possible to ask her what she has in mind. And I have no doubt at all that she'll have questions for me following her visit to Dan's bedroom this morning.

What shall I tell her? That he fucked me, and it was wonderful? Yes, I could say that much. That he's going to spank me for punching him yesterday, and I'm oddly calm at that prospect? Well yes, maybe I could say that too. That I'm starting to imagine him doing a whole lot more to me, and my pants get wet just thinking of it? Oh no, definitely not sharing that. Not yet anyway.

My head is whirling with the events of the last twenty-four hours, and for once that doesn't bother me unduly. I have no idea how I feel, except that it's broadly good. Dan both scares and excites me, and my stomach is churning as nervous, agitated butterflies seem to flutter their wings inside me. I really should have avoided the prawns—I suspect seafood and spanking will be a volatile combination for me. Still, too late now.

Is it disloyal to compare Dan and James? Possibly, but I can't help it. James' self-obsessed attempts at lovemaking versus Dan's intuitive sensitivity to my needs. James' clumsy fumblings only served to satisfy his own needs. He didn't even know I was faking orgasms. Dan's assured touch makes any thought of subterfuge both irrelevant and quite impossible. Dan would never be fooled by artful gasping and strategic clenching, not for a moment.

And what about those…others? The clients sent by my mother to my bedroom, men I serviced because it was easier that way, then got rid of, refusing even to look at their faces. Featureless, nameless, brutally erased from my memory, the details just a dark fog and better left that way. Even now, four years later, I still feel sick at the recollection, and there's nothing of the sensual butterfly in that. This is just plain ugly, humiliating, shameful. And buried. I've moved on.

"Are you alright, Summer?" Freya taps me on the arm and repeats the question, her hands swiftly forming the words. I shake myself, pulled from my reverie back into the present.

"Yes, yes of course. I was miles away. Sorry."

"Are you sure. You look pale." This from Eva. "Doesn't she, Dan?"

"Maybe. A little. Do you need some fresh air? A glass of water perhaps?" I turn to him in surprise. I never heard Dan approaching, but he's taken the empty seat next to me and is peering anxiously at me.

"I'm fine. Really. Just a bit tired, that's all. The traveling yesterday. Then the party, and it's been a long day…"

"Well, not yet it hasn't. I was going to ask you to dance with me, but if you're not up to it we can sit this one out."

"Oh no, you should dance. It's a wedding, and everyone has to dance at a wedding." Rosie sounds excited. She's just arrived at our table, Barney on her heels. She tugs at Dan's sleeve. "I'll dance with you, Uncle Dan."

"I'll hold you to that later. For now, could you take Barney outside please? He's not really allowed in here. And as for you, Miss Jones, are we dancing?"

"Are you asking?" I smile at him, my mood lightening.

"I'm asking."

"Then I'm dancing." He stands, holds out his hand.

I take it, and find myself drawn onto the dance floor. I'm not surprised to find Dan is an excellent dancer, another accomplishment to add to a growing list. His hold is possessive, comforting, assured but not restrictive. We whirl and glide through the crowd of other guests, and I seize the opportunity to wave to Ashley as she passes in Tom's arms, and again in Nathan's.

We've had no opportunity to chat today, and I don't expect we will. I'd been hoping to have more time with her though before she goes off on her honeymoon. There's still so much we need to catch up on.

"Have you enjoyed your day so far?" Dan's breath tickles my ear as he leans down to whisper to me.

"Yes. Very much. I'm so glad Ashley contacted me."

"Me too. So you enjoyed all of it? No second thoughts?"

He's referring to the events of this morning. And yesterday on the steps to Black Combe. And the consequences yet to be addressed. I look up at him to meet his gaze and shake my head. "No. None."

His smile is warm. "None so far. That's good. And later? After we finish here? I know I came on strong yesterday and you were feeling pressured, taken by surprise. I need you to understand that I'm not going to force anything on you that you don't want. Really don't want. You can say no. Always."

"I do know that." I think. I've yet to say no to Dan and make it stick. But I don't intend to try it tonight. "I accept what's coming. I trust you. And I want you to understand that I really am sorry for what happened. For all of it."

I'm referring to my bizarre behavior at the club all those months ago as well as the debacle yesterday, though I'm hoping Dan won't press me too hard to explain. Not here. Later perhaps, when we're alone.

"What's coming? Mmm, that's one way of putting it. I think you'll survive, though. I've not spent much time with you this afternoon. I'm sorry about that but it's been a bit manic."

"I know. And it's okay. I came to this wedding on my own. I don't expect you to…"

"You may have come here alone but you're not alone now." Dan interrupts my flow of words, and I fall silent. Considering. He steers us toward the edge of the dance floor and into a secluded niche beside a huge potted palm. He tips up my chin with his fingertips and brushes his lips over mine.

"You were Ashley's guest in the first place, now you're mine. Okay?"

"Your…guest?"

"Just…mine." He lowers his head to kiss me again, and there is no further conversation.

By seven in the evening I'm seriously flagging. Guests are starting to disperse, but there's still quite a crowd as we all troop outside to watch the fireworks. I'd expected Ashley and Tom to disappear off on honeymoon somewhere, but they're still here. According to Eva, Tom wants to oversee the initial stages of getting his wind farm scheme off the ground, so they've delayed their honeymoon for a couple of weeks. I'm glad, happy to have an opportunity to get to know Ashley all over again. Now that we're back in contact I intend to keep in touch, but emails and Facebook are no substitute for good old face-to-face girlie chats.

I've no firm plans for returning to Cumbria, but I suppose it'll be fairly soon. I'd wondered about scrounging a lift back to Kendall with Freya and Nick, but it seems they're also staying for a few more days. Nick intends to be at the wind farm meeting. I'm not sure my welcome will extend that far, after all, I hardly know Nathan and even if I am Dan's 'guest' it's his brother's house I'm staying in. What I do know is, I'm in no hurry to be away.

I wonder how long Dan will be here for?

My phone pings in my tiny clutch bag, signaling the arrival of a text. I'm surprised. Apart from Ashley, and now Freya, no one has my number. And they're both standing on either side of me. I reach into my bag to pull out the phone.

Time to go.

What the…? It's an unknown number. Well, in fairness all numbers are unknown as far as my phone's concerned. I peer at the message, then look up and glance around me. No clues. Nothing.

Another ping. I press the little orange icon to reveal the new message.

Behind you. Nathan's car.

I turn. Dan is lounging against the bonnet of Nathan's sleek black Porsche, the driver's door open. His phone is in his hand as he watches me from under lowered eyebrows. My stomach lurches, my pussy contracts, moistening. That look, pure Dom. He won't be kept waiting.

I turn to Freya. "I need to leave. I'll see you soon."

"What? But, where…?" She stops signing as her gaze follows mine. She sees Dan, and knows the score.

"Right. Later then. Have fun." She reaches up to kiss my cheek then turns back to the fireworks.

Fun? Maybe. Eventually. But first…

I walk slowly over to the Porsche, as Dan moves around the bonnet to open the passenger door.

Chapter Two

"Where are we going?"

I assumed we'd be headed back to Black Combe, but Dan drives straight past the junction leading up to Nathan and Eva's house and on toward Haworth.

"Leeds." Dan's answer is succinct, and he seems inclined to offer nothing more. I have visions of a club, or perhaps a hotel. I'm tired, I hope for the latter.

"Where in Leeds?" I glance quickly across at Dan, his hard profile outlined in the dim light from the dashboard.

He's a handsome man, devastatingly so, I'm fast appreciating, but his features now are stark, unrelenting. Gone is the gentle, playful lover who made love to me this morning and danced with me this afternoon. Here instead is the Dom bent on discipline, on teaching me obedience. And respect. I suspect I will learn those lessons well, no doubt starting with not questioning him. But still, I would like to know where we're headed.

"Please, Dan. Sir. I *would* like to know. Where are we going?"

He relents, perhaps in response to my polite inquiry. "Nathan's apartment in Leeds. You'll like it there. It's very well equipped."

So, not clubbing then. I'm pleased. An apartment sounds fine. Better than fine. Private. Peaceful. But I'm struck by Dan's odd choice of words.

"Well equipped? In what way?"

He shoots a swift, scornful glance in my direction before turning his attention back to the road. That look is enough, though, quite sufficient to clarify just what sort of equipment I might expect to encounter in Nathan Darke's apartment in Leeds.

Shit. I knew what was coming, but this makes it all so much more real.

"I see." I fold my hands in my lap and gaze out of the passenger window at the passing countryside. Or as much as I can see in the darkness. Dan offers no additional details, leaving me alone with my thoughts for now.

The journey passes quickly, the traffic is light at this time and Leeds is only about twenty-five miles away. Soon we're skirting the Bradford south ring road to pick up the motorway, and just minutes after that we're pulling off the slip road toward south Leeds. Dan negotiates the route confidently, his hands relaxed on the steering wheel. I find my eyes drawn to his long, strong fingers, my pussy dampening as I recall how they feel inside me. Soon, I hope.

He signals left and takes a sharp turn, steering the car into a small tunnel leading to an underground parking area. I guess we've arrived then. Dan pulls up in a parking bay sporting the initials 'ND'. He kills the engine and turns to me.

"Do you remember what I said to you about safe words? Back at the club in Lancaster?"

I don't pretend to misunderstand. "Yes. Red for stop, amber for slow down."

"Good. Use those any time you need to, really need to. Amber especially. I'll be happy to give you time, explain anything you need me to. Red's more serious. Use that only if you mean it. And, Summer, you don't have to go through with any of this, you do know that?"

"Yes, Sir, I understand." He made that perfectly clear on the dance floor. I accepted it then, and I still do.

"And? Still happy to be here? With me?"

Happy? Perhaps not quite yet. But happy enough. I nod briefly.

Dan gets out of the car, and before I can follow him he's come round to open my door for me. He offers me his hand to help me out, and I accept the unexpected chivalry. I've noticed this before, the strange juxtaposition of intimacy and humiliation with infinite respect and perfect courtesy. Dan is unfailingly polite and considerate. I recall he managed to remain so even as he strapped me, naked, to the spanking bench in Lancaster. He opens the car boot and pulls out a small overnight bag.

"A few things I asked Eva to pack for you. I hope you don't mind."

Mind? I'm struck again by his attention to detail, and to my comfort. It never occurred to me to ask to go and collect my things from Black Combe. "No, of course not. Thank you. I must thank Eva too, when we get back."

He shrugs and gestures for me to precede him to the lift. Dan punches a series of numbers into the keypad by the door, and within seconds a whirring sound heralds the imminent arrival of the lift. The doors glide apart, and I step inside. Dan follows, dropping my bag to the floor as he punches in another short series of numbers. The lift starts upwards, the motion smooth but it feels as though our ascent is rapid. I lean back against the wall of the lift, idly considering my reflection in the mirrored wall opposite. Dan is lounging alongside me, infinitely at ease. We're both still wearing our wedding finery, though Dan has long since discarded the tie, and his collar is unbuttoned. If anything, he looks even more attractive for being ever so slightly disheveled. My dress is creased across the front, so I smooth it out with my hands. Our eyes meet, reflected in the shiny metallic wall in front of us. The sardonic quirk to Dan's lips suggests he considers my attempts to restore order somewhat optimistic, but old habits die hard and I can do no other.

"Nice dress. Very sexy."

"Thank you, Sir. You look very nice too."

He smiles slightly, the only acknowledgment of my compliment. "Tell me, Miss Jones. How do you avoid a panty line in a dress so tight?"

I see my eyes widen in my reflected image, but I'm pleased to note my voice remains steady as I reply, "I'm wearing a thong, Sir."

"Ah yes, I thought so. May I have it please?" He holds out his hand, palm up.

I don't move. Forget to breathe.

"The thong, please. It would be better not to exacerbate your predicament by having me need to ask you a third time." His hand is still outstretched, waiting, but his tone now has an impatient edge to it, a subtle nuance but it makes me shiver.

And I know better than to waste any more time. I bend, lift the front of my skirt above my knees, and reach under to grab the front of my thong. I pull it down and step out of it, before handing the underwear to Dan. He thanks me politely and shoves the scrap of lace into his pocket before turning to the keypad again. This time the code he taps in causes the lift to shudder and stop.

He folds his arms across his chest, regarding my slightly startled expression in the mirrored wall. His eyes narrow, hardening to a deep, stone gray.

"You'll need to shimmy a little I imagine, but I want you to work that sexy little skirt way up high above your waist. Then I want you to turn and face the wall."

I gasp. "Here? In the lift?"

"Yes, Miss Jones. Here, in the lift. Get on with it please." He steps away from the wall, and reaches for the buckle on his belt. He unfastens it and starts to slide it through the loops in his dress trousers.

"Your belt? You mean to hit me with your belt?" I blurt out the obvious.

"I do, Miss Jones. Any objections?"

Yes! Plenty.

"No, Sir." I start to raise my skirt.

He's right about the shimmying, but the alternative is to remove my dress entirely, which I'd prefer not to do in a semi-public environment. A couple of minutes' wriggling and tugging see the silky fabric bunched around my waist and under my breasts. I'm naked from the waist down. Unless you count my thigh-high stockings and shoes of course, which Dan instructs me to leave in place. With an imperious whirl of his finger he instructs me to turn to the wall, baring my unprotected bottom.

"Lean on the wall—brace yourself against it. Now, arch your back and lift your bum up for me. Spread your legs a little more. Show me that pretty cunt of yours."

I adjust my position conscious of his eyes on me as I present myself for his punishment.

"Shoulders lower and back arched a little more, if you would please. Your body is beautiful, you can be proud of it. Show it off to me, girl."

His words have the desired effect. Far from feeling scared and humiliated, I do indeed know a sense of pride. I feel beautiful, desirable. Sexy and hot, and very, very wet now. I lean farther forward, consciously raising my bottom a little higher for his viewing.

"Turn your head — look at yourself in the mirror. See how gorgeous you are. You make me hard just looking at you, my sweet little fucktoy."

I do as I'm told, studying my body now reflected from the side, my naked bottom tilted upwards, my thighs parted. Dan is standing behind me, maybe three feet away, his belt now dangling from his hand. He's folded it, the buckle and other end grasped in his fist.

"How many stripes should I give you, do you think? How many have you deserved?"

"I don't know, Sir. Whatever you think..." But I hope it's not much. That belt looks as though it might sting a bit.

"You attacked me. I'm thinking ten, possibly twelve." His tone is dispassionate. He shifts his stance, swinging the belt as if he's about to start.

"No!" I blurt out my response, driven part by fear, but also by a sense of injustice. Yes, I hit him. But I didn't hurt him, and I have already apologized.

"No? No not at all, or no, not twelve?"

"I— Not twelve. Please."

"Ten?"

I whimper, my buttocks clenching pathetically.

"Eight?"

I drag in a deep breath and nod. "Yes, Sir, if you think so. Eight."

"You could accept eight, I know that. But we'll settle for six today. Three on each side. Are you ready for this?"

I nod again. "Yes, Sir. And, thank you." I am genuinely grateful for his consideration. He could have insisted on twelve strokes, I wouldn't have protested, though I might have been screaming 'red' well before the end.

"After each stroke I'll wait until you tell me you're ready, then I'll deliver the next one. So, the quicker you recover each time, the faster we'll be done with this. Do you understand?"

"Yes, Sir."

"No questions? No more negotiations?"

"No, Sir. Please, just do it."

"My pleasure, Miss Jones."

The soft whistle of the belt whizzing through the air is the only warning I get before the pain explodes across my left buttock. I scream, staggering under the shock, even though I know he didn't hit me especially hard. I'm shaking as I regain my balance, my arms braced against the cool metal wall.

"Miss Jones? Are you ready for me to continue?"

"Yes, Sir." I manage to force the words out through gritted teeth.

The belt whistles again, and this time my right buttock takes the hit. I scream, I can't help that, but the shock is less. This hurts like hell, but it *is* bearable. So far.

He waits patiently as I concentrate on breathing. He doesn't prompt me this time, and I manage to gather my wits enough to ask him to proceed.

"I'm ready. Aagh!"

He wastes no time in applying the belt again, the second blow to my left buttock, just below the previous one. I know the tears are now streaming down my face, but I'm half way there and not giving in now. I stiffen my legs, lock my knees under me.

"Please continue, Sir." I manage to gasp out the words.

"Thank you, Miss Jones. You're doing very well, by the way."

My polite acknowledgment of his compliment is lost as the fourth stroke connects with my right buttock, the sharp crack resounding around the small lift car. I scream, of course, but manage not to move. Or I think I haven't.

"I'm going to lay the last two across your upper thighs. You'll find it painful to sit for a day or two, which is intentional. This is a punishment, after all, Miss Jones, and I want you to remember it. So, drop your shoulders please and lift your bottom up. I want a clear shot."

I moan softly, but follow his instructions, leaning farther down and deliberately raising my bottom up to give him ready access to the backs of my legs.

"Say when, Miss Jones." His voice is low, but quite implacable. Something tells me these last two will really hurt.

"Now. Please, just do it, do both and let me get up." I've given up trying to sound brave. I can hear the tremor in my voice, so he must too. Now, I just want this to be over. I need it to be over.

"Happy to oblige. You can thank me afterwards."

The sound of the belt whooshing through the air warns me, and I clench up solid in anticipation of the blow. I am not disappointed, and scream in real agony as my left thigh feels to be on fire.

"Oh, God. Please, that hurts…"

"Last one, Summer. Accept it, then we're done."

I don't answer, can't verbalize anything in this moment. Instead I nod frantically. It's enough. I open my eyes in time to see his feet reflected in the mirrored wall. He shifts his stance, the belt whistles one last time before landing across my right thigh. The pain explodes, my knees buckle, and I would have been on the floor but for Dan's arm suddenly encircling my waist and holding me upright.

"Steady. Lean on the wall and don't move yet."

"Please, can I stand up? We've finished." I'm whimpering, I know it. But I don't care.

"We have finished, but I want you to stay there a little longer please."

Obedient, I lay my forehead against the cool metal in front of me, heaving great, noisy sighs as my body adjusts to this latest turn of events. *What now?*

Dan allows me a few moments to recover. Then, "Open your eyes, Summer. Look at me."

With some effort I pry open my eyelids, turning my head to see Dan crouching beside me. His face is below mine, his eyes beautiful in the harsh strip lights, his expression soft and infinitely caring. He smiles, and I'm amazed to realize I'm smiling back. It's a watery effort, but surely it's the thought that counts. Dan seems to think so, at least as he reaches up to stroke my wet cheek.

There's a sharp snap, then, "Here, take a drink." He places an opened bottle of mineral water against my lips, tilting it for me to drink. The cool liquid is wonderful, refreshing in my dry mouth. I gulp it gratefully, wrapping my hand around his to hold the bottle in place.

"There's plenty more inside. I just want you to see this. Look at your reflection."

"How? I mean, where…?"

He stands, places his hands on my shoulders to ease me away from the wall. "Look up. Look at you."

I lift my chin to see my own tear-stained face looking back at me. Then, as I gaze at my reflection, I see more. Reflected in the opposite wall I see my own bum, perfectly poised still as if for the spanking, but now sporting vivid red stripes, two on each cheek and one across each of my thighs just above the top of my stockings. The contrast is sharp, painful against my pale skin. My beautiful swallows complete the tableau, soaring gracefully up the edge of my right buttock as if about to alight on their new perches.

"Oh." I can only gasp.

"Tell me." Dan clearly wants more. His tone is insistent, Dom style.

"I look— It looks…sore. And sexy. Very sexy."

"Yes, both those things. Anything else?"

"I want you to fuck me. Please. Now, Sir."

He slips his fingers between my buttocks, and seems to be taking care to avoid the sore places as he slides down to plunge two slick digits deep inside me. The sound of wet and ready pussy is sensual, adding to my arousal. I groan, gripping his fingers tightly.

"Yes, oh yes. That feels good. More please, could you…?"

He withdraws his fingers, and this time does lightly pat my sore bum. I shriek, as much in frustration as pain.

"Soon, my gorgeous little fucktoy. Inside. Where I can take a bit more time and trouble over you. Be patient, stand up now and straighten your clothes."

"But..." My protest dies on my lips as his expression brooks no argument.

He keys in another code on the keypad, and the lift whirs back into life. It takes me by surprise—I'd actually forgotten where we are. Moments later the doors are gliding silently open, and I'm still struggling to right my dress as he picks up my holdall and steps out. I stumble after him, my bottom rubbing painfully against the tight fabric of my skirt. Dan turns, takes my arm to steady me. I cling onto him as we cross the thickly carpeted foyer toward the one door that seems to open off this landing. I glance around, curious. Freya's place is grand, but this is on another scale entirely.

The knee-deep shag-pile is just the beginning. The walls are lined in what looks to me like marble paneling, and there are pieces of expensive looking art strategically displayed on small pedestal tables. I spot an alabaster bowl, backlit to better display its translucent beauty, and a carved wooden bird, an eagle maybe, is perching majestically in the center of the space.

"Do these things belong to Nathan? Is he a collector?"

Dan turns to me as he slides a key card into the slot on the door opposite the lift. "Nathan? No. This stuff started appearing when Eva moved in. It's her influence at work. Nathan likes pretty things, but he prefers them to have a pulse. I tend to agree." He opens the door, then stands aside to gesture me to go in.

The apartment is stunning too, but in a much more austere and utilitarian way. Sleek, gleaming, functional. I suspect Eva's influence has its limits, or maybe she just doesn't want to bother with interior decor. Not that the place needs it. The space is open-plan, a huge living area in the center with a dining zone at one end, near the kitchen. The large dining table seats eight easily, and I wonder if Nathan does much entertaining here. Apart from the obvious.

As I turn slowly, taking in my surroundings, Dan dumps my bag on a sofa.

"You can look round later—I'll do you the grand tour. Now, though, lose the dress. And the rest. I want you naked, and on your knees."

I snap out of my silent appraisal and reach for my zipper. "Yes, Sir."

He watches me struggle for a few moments before stepping behind me to slide the zip down. Then he steps back to watch as I peel the pale blue fabric gingerly down over my sore bum to lay it neatly on the sofa next to my bag. That dress cost me a lot of money, I intend to wear it again. I reach behind me to unclasp my bra and remove that too before stepping out of my spiky black shoes. They also cost a fortune. I really pushed the boat out for Ashley's big day.

I finish by slowly rolling down my stockings and depositing those on my pile of clothing. Nude, I glance back at Dan for more instructions. Where would he like me to kneel?

By way of an answer he points to the spot right in front of him. I walk over there, and drop to my knees on the floor.

"I seem to recall you said you wouldn't kneel at my feet."

"That was before."

"Before?"

"Before you promised to fuck me. And to take plenty of time over it. Only, not too much time, if you wouldn't mind. Sir."

He chuckles, reaching out to trail his fingers through my hair. "How impatient you've become. But you'll have to wait a little longer. Do you know what this is, Summer?"

He reaches into his jacket pocket with his free hand and pulls out a small object. It's vaguely cylindrical but with a narrow band close to one end, and made of some sort of plastic I'd say. It's a rather fetching shade of lemon yellow. I look at it, then shake my head slowly.

"No, Sir. Should I recognize it?"

"Not necessarily. It's a butt plug, Summer. And I think you know where it's going. Don't you?"

"Sir? I've never…" I've been managing to keep my eyes downcast, but I almost crick my neck as I tip up my chin to stare at him. I mean, I knew about anal play, but I thought we'd work up to it a little more slowly.

"I know you haven't. But you have to start somewhere, and it might as well be here. Now. With this. I chose a small one for you, in deference to your sweet little virgin arse."

"I see." Said virgin arse is clenching desperately. I might throw up.

"You can thank me for my kindness and consideration if you like."

"Do I have to, Sir?"

"Do you have to thank me? Or do you have to accept the butt plug?"

"Well, either I suppose." I know I'm sounding vaguely mutinous, but really, this is all moving very fast. He's thrashed me with a belt, and I managed to accept that. I've stripped on command and knelt at his feet. I'd expected things to become a little less challenging from here, but instead he piles on the pressure.

"Thanks are a matter for your own discretion. The butt plug's not optional. But it won't hurt you either. You *can* do this, Summer. And you can do it the easy way if you choose to." His clipped tone is not terribly encouraging, especially when he points to the floor, indicating that I should drop my gaze.

I try to inject a suitable note of compliance into my next question. "Which is what, Sir?"

"You can lean forward, put your forehead on the floor and your bum in the air. Arch your back for me like I taught you in the lift. Then you can reach back and hold your buttocks apart while I lube you up. Then, when I tell you to, you can bear down while I slide this in. Nice and easy."

"Easy for you maybe. And the hard way?" Too late, I try to bite back the insubordinate tone, but mercifully he doesn't pick up on it. I know I need to watch that, though — it will do me no good.

"You can make a fuss, tense up, squeeze your arse shut and try to prevent me getting in. If you ask me to stop, you know I will. I'll never force you to do anything. But I want you to do this, and if you want to please me, you will. And you'll do it willingly, without protest. Do your best to help. And one last thing, Summer. Your body will have no trouble at all accepting this, once your head stops fighting. This is about surrender. Are you ready for that?"

"I'm not sure, Sir." That's the truth at least.

"Well, we'll soon know. Lean forward, please."

And I do. I actually stop protesting and I do it.

Dan walks behind me and crouches. I flinch as he caresses my left buttock, the red stripes still making themselves felt despite his gentle touch. But the pain is nowhere near as severe as I imagined it would be.

"Reach back with both hands and hold your butt cheeks apart if you would please."

Ah, so polite. Wordless, I do as he asks. The slick coolness of the lubricant is oddly pleasant as he squirts it directly onto my exposed anus. I suppose he must have had that in his pocket too, though I don't ask him. I'm too concerned right now with the unsettling sensation of having the lube worked into the delicate skin around my arse, and even inside the rim. I gasp as he slips one finger in, swirling it to smear the goo all around. He withdraws his finger, only to replace it with what I assume is the nozzle of the tube. He squeezes a generous amount directly inside me, and I squeal.

"Wimp. That didn't hurt."

I clench my bum in automatic self-defense, consciously loosening the tight muscle as he places his fingertip at the entrance again. I don't want to resist, and I'm oddly reluctant to attract any fresh censure, no matter how gentle. "No, Sir. I'm sorry. It feels odd though."

"Odd nasty or odd nice?" His words are accompanied by the penetration of one well-oiled finger, sliding easily inside my bum.

"Oh, Sir."

I can't help my startled moan, and he takes advantage of my apparent acquiescence to finger-fuck my arse. He isn't rough with me, and is very deft about it, working the sphincter open to accept his presence more readily. I have to admit, he does seem very good at this, and he was right about my body accepting what's happening. It feels strange, and distinctly humiliating, but it's definitely not painful. Well, not yet. I start to revise that view as he inserts a second finger alongside the first. Now it's tight, I feel stretched, less comfortable. Hurting. Getting scared.

"Tell me, Summer."

"Tell you what, Sir?"

"Tell me."

"It hurts, Sir. It's scaring me now."

"We slow down then. You were okay with one finger, right?"

"Yes, Sir. One was fine."

"Like this?"

My body relaxes immediately as he reverts to just one finger, sliding it deep inside me and out again, each thrust hard and strong but no longer painful. I'm amazed, it was so easy. All I had to do was tell him.

"Okay now? Does that feel good?"

"Yes, Sir." And it does. Incredible though that may be, it really does.

He shifts, reaching around and under me to strum my clit with his other hand. I groan my appreciation as my orgasm begins to unfurl. Helpless to resist, my pussy spasms in response as I lay my cheek flat against the rug under me. Dan takes that as his cue to up the ante once more, and slides that second finger into my arse again. This time, though, I'm fine. Bolstered by Dan's quiet, confident efficiency, I'm even managing to relax and though it's still tight there's no sense of panic now. I gasp, but a couple of well-directed flicks across the tip of my clit soon restore orgasmic order. Moments later I'm climaxing hard.

Dan continues to thrust his fingers into my bum until the final waves of my release settle. He then pulls out, but only for a moment. Within seconds the cool hard surface of the butt plug presses against my now unresisting arse. It's cool, but smooth, and less wide than his two fingers had been. It slides into my well lubricated and loosened arse with remarkable ease. My ring of muscle tightens around the narrow section, holding it in place. Dan circles my bum with his fingertip, nudging the protruding part of the plug to cause it to move inside me. I'm intensely aware of it, of each rocking, swirling motion. I groan, sinking my fingers into the deep pile of the rug. Dan gives the plug a couple of experimental tugs to ensure it's not going anywhere. Then he stands and walks away from me. I hear running water, and crack open my eyes to see him washing his hands at the sink in the kitchen alcove. He finishes then turns to face me, a towel in his hands. He's regarding me, his expression cold. I'm struck by how handsome, and how powerful he looks, towering there still fully dressed in his smart wedding finery. Whilst I grovel on the floor in front of him, naked, humiliated. And so aroused I could weep.

"Are you in pain, Summer?"

"No, Sir. I'm fine." I mumble my answer through my disheveled hair but he hears me.

"In that case, what are you doing still on the floor? Kneel up. Now." His tone is curt, and my contrition is instant.

I try to push myself back onto my knees, but each movement brings a wave of rather odd sensation deep inside my arse. Not unpleasant, but very, very unsettling. I'm not in pain, but still feeling delicate. At last, though, I'm back on my knees, my hands laid on my thighs palms up, my eyes directed toward a spot on the floor about a foot in front of me. And it's that spot that Dan chooses to plant his feet as he comes back to stand over me.

"Look up, Summer. Look at me."

I obey, regarding him through a shimmer of tears. I'm not sure why I'm crying. Maybe I'm not—not really. It's just all so, so…overwhelming. He sees my emotions painted across my face. Of course he sees. He misses nothing. He crouches, now at my eye level. He wipes away a tear from my cheek with the pad of his thumb, but makes no other comment.

"Now for the fucking part. You were looking forward to that I think, my sweet little slut. Are you still of the same mind?"

I blink, shake my head briefly in an attempt to clear my vision if not my thinking.

"Yes, Sir. Please."

He smiles as he cups my chin with his hand. "Good. You've done well this evening. I know that wasn't easy, and I can tell by your face it still isn't. But you haven't whinged, haven't complained. I'm very impressed. You deserve something nice now. Go into the bedroom and wait for me there please."

He gestures with his head to a point somewhere behind me, presumably the bedroom, though I've yet to enjoy the grand tour. I was hardly through the door into the apartment before he ordered me to strip and kneel.

Obedient, I start to rise, but find this is not easy. Each time I move, so does the plug, sending waves of sensation through my arse. My cunt clenches, the hardness of the plug pressing against the soft walls of my pussy. I stagger as I try to stand, and might have dropped back to my knees but for Dan's steadying hands under my elbows. Despite his chilled sharpness when he spoke to me a few moments ago he's all concerned kindness now, gently easing me onto my feet. I cling to his arms, aware once more of his pristine fully dressed elegance in sharp contrast to my own state of naked vulnerability.

But I feel safe. Totally safe. And very enthusiastic about what's to come.

"Go on. I'll be with you in a minute." He turns me and points to a door across the room. He drops a kiss onto my shoulder and pats my still tender bum.

And I start to move. My progress is slow, decidedly unsteady, but I'm determined to get to the bedroom. As he says, I've earned it. As I reach the door Dan calls his final instructions to me.

"Face down on the bed. There are restraints on the headboard. Please slip those around your wrists and I'll tighten them in a moment."

Chapter Three

Two things strike me immediately as I enter the bedroom—two dominant features. First, the bed, which is huge and looks to be made of solid oak does indeed sport leather straps attached to the headboard. It is oddly positioned in the center of the room. A large chest, also oak by the look of it, sits at its foot. The duvet is a plain, deep red which matches the carpet.

The second striking feature is the St Andrew's Cross positioned against one wall, huge and sturdy and constructed of a dark, warm looking wood. The last time I saw one of those my friend Freya was strapped to it, naked and blindfolded, in the club in Lancaster. I have a strong suspicion I will become intimately acquainted with the capabilities of this particular item of equipment myself, if not this visit then soon. But not now. Not immediately. Dan promised me something rather nicer. I turn my back on the cross and, courtesy of the plug nestled conspicuously in my bum, clamber somewhat awkwardly onto the bed.

I only just have time to wriggle into position, my wrists threaded through the loose leather straps, as Dan enters the room. He closes the door behind him then leans against it to survey me. I turn my head to look at him, uncertain whether I should smile, speak, make eye contact or what.

Dan settles the matter by flashing me a dazzling smile. "You look absolutely beautiful, your bottom striped from my belt, my plug up your arse."

"I, I feel good. Sir. I think."

"You think?"

"A little sore. Your belt is heavy, Sir, and I didn't like having the plug put in. But I'm glad I did it. *We* did it, I mean..."

"You can thank me if you like, for my time and attention in teaching you how to do these things. And if you'd like to offer your apology again for yesterday's display on my brother's front step now might be a good time." His smile is warm as he strides across the room toward me, despite his stern words. And it all seems so easy, suddenly.

"Yes, Sir. Thank you, for teaching me. And for helping me. And especially for slowing down when I was finding it hard. I did appreciate that, really. And I am truly sorry for what happened yesterday. I can't believe I did such a thing. It's just not me, it really isn't. Even before you beat me with your belt I was deeply ashamed."

He sits beside me, trails his fingers slowly across my shoulder and down my spine. It feels wonderfully sensual and I raise my hips as he reaches my bottom. Maddeningly, he stops there. "You've accepted your fault, and your punishment." He traces the lines on my bottom by way of emphasizing his point. "And I get the impression you've learnt from the experience.

There's no need for you to feel ashamed now. It's done. We've moved on. It's what you do from here that matters, not what happened in the past."

If only everything could be so simple.

"Thank you, Sir." I whisper my response as he continues to caress my throbbing buttocks. He reaches for the straps to tighten them around my wrists then seems to think better of it.

"I've changed my mind. I think I'd prefer you on your back. Roll over please."

I do so without hesitation, although the pressure on my bottom as I settle my weight again is uncomfortable, both inside and out. Without waiting for his instruction I place my hands back in the restraints, and this time he tightens them around my wrists. He tests the fit to make sure I'm securely held but my circulation is not compromised. Needless to say, he is entirely satisfied on both counts.

"Lift your bum up please."

I do as he asked, and he shoves two pillows under me, raising my hips up off the bed. I hiss with the sharp pain as my tender bum rubs against the crisp, freshly laundered cotton of the pillowcases. He quirks his lip in wry acknowledgment, but he says nothing more on the subject of my delicate condition. Instead, he's ready to get on with the real business of why we are here. "Open your legs. I want to check if you're still ready for me."

I suspect there's little doubt on that particular score, but I spread my thighs dutifully. I'm every bit as keen as he seems to be to make progress. More so perhaps.

He draws a long, slow, open-handed caress along my pussy, from front to back. His fingertips slide between my folds and he manages to dip the end of his middle finger into my cunt as he passes. It feels wonderful, the caress intimately casual, and I groan my approval.

"Mmm, what a randy little slut you are, Miss Jones. And so tight, just as I remember noticing this morning. So wet and hot too. Have I been keeping you waiting by any chance?"

"That's quite alright, Sir. But if you wouldn't mind perhaps…" Two can play at being polite. Well, for a while at least. I'm in imminent danger of forgetting my manners entirely as he slips three fingers into my slick cunt and thrusts hard.

"Oh, God. Sir! Please."

"Okay, Miss Jones, I get the message." He pulls his fingers out of me and stands, grinning at my obvious discomfort and impatience as he slowly unbuttons his dress shirt.

He removed his cuff links earlier and rolled up his sleeves to deal with my virgin bum, but now he slips off the shirt and drops it on top of the chest at the foot of the bed. I'm struck again by the sheer masculine perfection of his torso, the firm planes of his muscles as he moves around the room, adjusting lamps and unzipping his gray trousers. His skin is a darker shade than mine, his forearms maybe slightly more tanned than the rest of him, suggesting he spends a lot of time outdoors with his sleeves rolled up. I suppose zoo vets have to go to their patients—it would be tricky getting a giraffe into the compact surgery at the animal park.

I forget to breathe for a few moments as he drops his trousers and dumps them on the chest too. He isn't wearing socks or shoes, so I assume he left them out in the living room. In just his boxers, which are made of some sort of silky, shiny fabric, his erection looks immense, jutting out, tenting his pants. If I was not tied to the bed I would be unable to resist tugging the waistband down to reveal it, maybe even sink to my knees at his feet again, this time to suck on it. But all of that is not to be. I can only lie here and watch and wait.

Dan settles himself alongside me on the bed, propped up on his elbow as he looks down at me, spread out for his use.

"Christ, you are utterly lovely. So sexy, so perfectly submissive. Where have you been hiding all this?"

I don't know if he expects an answer to that, but I have no chance in any case. He dips his head to take my nipple in his mouth and sucks on it gently. Instinctively I tense, expecting to feel the pinch of his teeth, anticipating the sharp tang of pleasure mixed with pain which I now associate with Dan's touch. It doesn't happen. His lips are achingly tender as he rubs them across my sensitive peaks, first one, then the other. He settles in, using his tongue to deepen the caress. I gasp, arching my back. Without releasing my nipple, Dan slips his hand between my thighs again and takes hold of the finger grip on the butt plug. He shakes it lightly, sending ripples of pure sensation pulsating through my arse. It feels good. Odd, but good. Better than good even as the sweetly intimate vibration tingles inside me. Amazing what my body can do, can accept and achieve once my head stops its puritanical finger-wagging.

And talking of fingers, Dan's are busy. He slides three of them deep into my pussy, pressing hard against the butt plug filling my rear channel whilst angling his hand so that the heel of it is resting on my clit. He rubs hard, scissoring his fingers inside my cunt as he does so. My orgasm hits out of almost nowhere, surging up and overwhelming me in seconds under his unrelenting caresses. My nipples, my clit, my pussy, my arse, all are engaged and sensuously connected. The sensations sizzle through me as I writhe under him, stretching against the restraints but with no wish at all to be free. Being bound removes all inhibitions, as though none of this is under my control. Which of course it isn't, as long as I leave my safe words conveniently out of it. Red and amber can mind their own business for now. I'm having fun, lots of fun, and it seems that Dan's only mission at this moment is to deliver plenty more of the same.

He releases my nipple as the tremors of orgasm slide away and my body stills again. Shifting his position he trails a line of nibbling little kisses down my stomach to my pale colored, tight pubic hair. He mutters something which sounds a bit like 'natural blonde' as he noses his way through the soft curls, but by now I think most of the blood has rushed to my clit and nothing from my neck up works that well. I couldn't care less, only intent on lifting my hips to allow him better access. He takes the hint, for once not making me wait or beg or even ask nicely. He takes my swollen, throbbing clit between his lips and holds it there as he flicks the tip with his tongue. It's a delightfully effective little trick, quite a party piece in fact as I come again, instantly. This time my release is even more powerful, my entire body shaking as the waves of ecstasy roll through me, from my hot, throbbing core and away through my outstretched limbs. I hear a voice, which has to be mine because Dan's mouth is completely occupied.

"Oh God. Oh God. Oh…"

His fingers are inside me again—just two, I think, sliding in and out. Fast. He hits my G-spot each time, drawing out the pleasure. One orgasm? Maybe. Or it could be several, one after the other. Who knows? Who cares? I shake and moan and throb and thrust my hips, and Dan does the rest.

At last he stops. Or allows me to stop. I'm spent, floppy as a wet dishcloth, my eyes closed as I concentrate on drawing in some much-needed oxygen. I'm only vaguely aware of the sound of foil snapping, the bed shifting under Dan's weight as he moves. I lie still, utterly relaxed, convinced that at some stage soon the room will stop spinning. Or maybe just the bed will. Either would be fine.

"Open your eyes, my little slut."

"I can't," I murmur my protest, sure that even lifting one eyelid is quite beyond me.

He responds by slipping the head of his cock into my pussy, stretching my entrance but not pressing home. That gets my attention and my eyes shoot open. He is poised above me, his soft smile both sexy and caring. How can he manage to combine rampant lust with aching tenderness? I can't fathom it, but he does, and in a way which is uniquely him.

I smile back. It seems appropriate. He shifts, and plunges forward to plant his cock deep inside me.

My head is thrown back in silent appreciation, and he takes the opportunity to sink deep, open-mouthed kisses into my neck. He reaches up to cover my still bound hands in his, lacing his fingers through mine. As he draws his hands and mine back down the bed I realize that I'm free, and in a sudden and unexpected burst of energetic enthusiasm I push against him. He takes the hint immediately and rolls onto his back, pulling me on top. For once I have the opportunity to be the aggressor, to be active, to take the lead. I relish my unaccustomed freedom, straddling him and bracing my knees on the bed in order to pump my hips up and down. My erratic motion lacks Dan's practiced ease, but is effective even so. I squeeze my pussy around him, loving the feeling of fullness each time I sink down on his shaft, the sense that I am stretched and somehow re-formed around him. Remade to fit him exactly. In every way.

Heady stuff, and my mind is reeling almost as much as my body as I gyrate my hips and thrust ever more frantically. Dan reaches down, takes the finger grip of the butt plug in his hand again and shakes it sharply. It feels incredible, rammed up hard and tight against his huge cock, just a slender and sweetly sensitive piece of my body separating the two. I can feel him, everywhere, in every way.

I use my hands to press against his chest and push myself upright. I glance down at him through half-closed eyelids, my breasts now jiggling prettily in front of his face. That fact seems not to be lost on him as he leans forward to lick each of my nipples in turn. He lies back, his grin pure sensuality now. His right hand continues to swirl the butt plug inside me as his left slides between us to caress my clit again. And I lose it. I'm flying, in orbit, shaking, convulsing, spasming around his cock as my orgasm ricochets through me again. I might be screaming. Someone is. The sound continues, lowering to a deep, contented moan as the sensations subside to just a delicious, satisfying flutter of nerve endings re-aligning themselves.

As my climax fades I'm aware of Dan's low moan, more a growl perhaps. His hands are on my hips, holding me in place as he thrusts upwards. His movements are sharp, driving fully into me. His cock twitches hard, the guttural sounds deep in his throat a clear indication that he is also close. I squeeze my muscles around him, roll my hips in a slowly, deliberate motion, instinctively seeking to offer whatever will enhance his pleasure. He clasps me around the waist, holding me close against him as he lurches his upper body up to press his chest against my breasts. One final spearing movement and his cock is buried in me to the hilt. He goes still, holding me motionless as his hot semen fills my pussy.

When he relaxes his grip and sinks back onto the mattress I fall forward, my breasts pressed against Dan's chest. He takes that opportunity to give the butt plug a sharp tug, and I gasp once more as it pops out. Dan tosses it onto the floor before wrapping his arms around me.

"It's your job to clean that. Later."

I snuggle against him, loving the feel of his cock still buried deep inside me. It's an intimate moment, deeply personal. Maybe Dan feels it too as he doesn't rush to disengage, just allows me to sag against him and drink in the contented bliss of an exquisite experience shared.

All good things must end, though, and at last he places his hands on my hips to gently lift me from him. I murmur my discontent, but he ignores me. He quickly removes the condom and drops that next to the butt plug — another of my jobs perhaps? Then he somehow shifts us both to free the duvet from underneath us. He pulls me back on top of him to hold me close again, dragging the quilt over us.

And that's all I remember.

* * * *

I wake up early the next morning, pleasantly stiff, to find Dan Riche snuggled up close to my back. He's warm, hard and solid, his arm slung loosely across my ribs anchoring me in place. I wriggle backwards, easing closer to him, and his arm tightens. His fingers brush my breast, the caress sensual even in sleep. I lie in blissful remembering, reliving each moment of last night's encounter. The soaring heights and the more challenging bits. With the distance of a few hours' sleep, and when set next to the unbelievable intensity of the orgasms he gave me, even the humiliation of having the butt plug inserted seems trivial now. He couldn't have taken me to those heights, I suspect, had he not previously scared me, jarred my senses. Mastered my resistance.

I'm beginning to understand, maybe a little, what submission means. What this lifestyle offers. What it was that Freya found, and once discovered wouldn't let go no matter what the disappointments along the way. It's a powerful discovery, liberating even. I lie on my side, listening to Dan's quiet breathing behind me. I'm content to be still, to just wait, and...

I catch sight of the discarded butt plug and condom still lying on the floor alongside the bed. I stare at them, remembering Dan's words from yesterday. 'Your job'. I was supposed to tidy things up. I didn't. Nothing so remarkable there perhaps. I was tired after all. With good reason. And comfortable, content to just drift off to sleep. So I left them.

I left them there. Me, I left the mess there, just forgot about it and went to sleep. Me, the compulsive tidier. Me, the sad person who packs her bag with meticulous care and only yesterday morning spent ten minutes straightening the toiletries in Dan's bathroom cabinet while he waited for me in his bedroom. I just fell asleep. As if none of it mattered, as if it could all wait till morning.

Which of course it could, if you were anyone but me. Everyone else would do just as I did and think nothing of it. But that's not me, I know something is different. Something's changing. My values, my habits, my beliefs. My priorities. And on that note, my bladder makes its presence felt. I need the loo. I ease myself out from under Dan's possessive arm as carefully as I can, not wanting to wake him. Extricated, I slip from the bed, stop to pick up the items on the floor, then head across to the door in the corner which I assume must house the en suite facilities.

It does, and I quickly accomplish what's necessary. I leave the butt plug to dry on the windowsill, not sure where Dan—or Nathan—usually keeps such things, then emerge intending to slide back into bed. I decide instead to go on a coffee hunt. My bag is still out in the living room so I borrow a large bathrobe I find hanging on the back of the door and pad barefoot out of the bedroom.

It only takes a few minutes to locate the coffee and a cup, and soon I'm seated on the arm of the sofa, looking out of the huge picture windows at the Leeds skyline, hugging a mug of steaming, black, heavily sweetened caffeine. There's no milk in the fridge so I have to manage without that. I can see that this apartment block is set among other similar buildings, ranged along the banks of a river. The Aire? The development is clearly some sort of shopping or tourist destination as well as up-market apartments, with designer shops and eateries. Pizza Express, a tapas bar, a casino.

I can even see a Tesco Express at the end of the row—they'd have milk. I could throw some clothes on and nip down there.

I'm digging through my bag for underwear when Dan ambles out of the bedroom, clearly lured by the aroma of my finest instant coffee.

"Morning, beautiful. I wondered where you'd got to."

"I needed the loo. And some coffee. I was just about to go out for some milk."

"No need. It'll have been delivered by now. Did you check in the lobby?" He drops a kiss on the top of my head as he strolls past to grab a mug from the cupboard.

"The lobby? No. Should I?"

"Yup. I phoned ahead yesterday, asked security to leave us a few essentials. They should have been brought up overnight. The key card's on the table by the door. Would you mind checking?"

I pad over there and open the door. Sure enough, in a neat cardboard box outside the door, are a collection of groceries, plus a copy of yesterday's Horse Racing News. I heft the box up and bring it back inside with me. I dump it on the kitchen worktop, and pull out the newspaper.

"Yours?"

He takes it from my outstretched hand. "Yes. Thanks. I never had time to get a copy yesterday. Meant to nip out first thing, before the wedding, but I was waylaid." He grins at me in a manner I could only describe as lecherous, and my pussy starts its habitual clenching and moistening at the mere mention of yesterday's fun and games. Ho hum.

"Are you keen on racing then?" I'm thinking he and Freya might have a lot in common, what with her newly discovered fondness for matters of the turf. And buying racehorses.

"More of a professional interest, though I do enjoy an occasional flutter." He puts his mug down to open the paper, spreading it out on the worktop. You already know I'm a vet, specializing in exotics and large animals. The zoo, obviously, that's one of my jobs, and I do some work with farm animals though not a great deal. I'm also one of the course vets at Cartmel, hence..." He gestures to the racing journal.

"Oh. Right. I see. Racing and zoos? Sounds fascinating."

"Hmm, sometimes. It has its glamorous side I suppose but I spend most of my time on a race day doing random blood tests and peering at hooves. There's the occasional drama, but that's not usually of a pleasant nature."

"Oh, right. I suppose not. Do you prefer the zoo then?"

"It's just different. Lots more variety, obviously. I get to deal with rhino diarrhea and giraffe laryngitis..."

"That'd be a tall order..."

"Ha ha. Good one. I'll write it down. Is there any milk in that box?

I hand him the carton. "So you don't do cats and dogs then?"

"Not as a rule. Some wildlife occasionally. Members of the public quite often bring injured hedgehogs and such things to the park. The occasional badger..." He flashes me a wry grin. "If I'm around I do some patching up before handing them on to the RSPCA."

I regard him with renewed respect. I'd been so glad of his help the night I ran over Bryan the badger, but I didn't appreciate that he regularly did such freebies for animals that had no one else to help them. This is a humanitarian side to Dan Riche I hadn't really suspected. He catches my astonished expression.

"Why look so surprised. Just because I gave you a hard time doesn't mean I'm not nice to little furry creatures. Is there anything to eat in that box?"

"Cereals. A few of those little individual packets. And some bread. We could make toast. And, you didn't give me a hard time. Not really."

"No? I'm slacking then. What about eggs? Bacon?"

I double check, but I'm not optimistic. "No. Nothing like that. I saw a Tesco down by the dock. I could go down there?"

"No, it's alright. Toast will be fine. Do we have butter?"

I slap the small carton on the worktop. "Can I ask you something? Something that's been puzzling me for a long time?" Dan's reference to Bryan has reminded me of that day, our very first meeting.

Dan lifts one eyebrow as he pulls the lid off the plastic container. "Go ahead."

"The day I brought the badger to the zoo, you said you wanted to spank me. Do you always say things like that to perfect strangers?"

Dan puts the butter down and fixes his undivided attention on me. "As I recall, I offered to spank you, I agree the difference is subtle, but it's there even so."

"Why? Why did you say that? How did you know?"

"Know what? That you were a submissive and would respond to it?"

"I suppose so. Because I wasn't, not then. I mean, if I was, I didn't know."

"I knew. The clues were there. You called me sir without thinking, you kept lowering your eyes every time I looked directly at you or asked you a question. Your whole demeanor screamed submissive. It was instinctive, and so was my reaction. Your response to my offer clinched it."

"I turned you down flat!"

"So you did. But you still let me kiss you at the gate."

"I didn't let you. You just—did it."

Dan's grin is nothing short of lecherous. "You could have stopped me. You *did* stop me—eventually."

I nod. "Then you apologized. And you asked me to dinner."

"And again, you turned me down flat."

"I wish I hadn't."

"Oh? You weren't entirely repulsed by my suggestions then? The spanking I mean, not dinner."

I shake my head. "I was shocked. Stunned. As for the dinner invitation, when I thought about it afterwards, I wasn't sure you were even serious. I mean, you could have had dinner with anyone you wanted." I didn't intend to tell him that, but somehow the words just slipped out. It's true though. Over the years since I'd often wondered what might have happened if I'd been able to find the courage to accept an invitation from a handsome vet. To take a risk. I never forgot him, though, my road not taken.

"I wanted you."

"You wanted to spank me. That terrified me back then."

"Not now?"

"No." I hesitate for a moment, then, "For ages after, I wished I'd gone to dinner with you."

He smiles at me, lifts his hand to cup my cheek. "Me too. But it's turned out okay. Dinner would have been nice, but if I had to choose, I'm even more pleased we're having breakfast together."

Dan winks at me. "And speaking of which, will cereals and toast suit you? Then a long soak in my brother's bubble bath. You'll like that. And if you're still stiff after the Jacuzzi you get one of my patented massages. Never fails to loosen up aching submissives."

The massage does sound rather nice. The Jacuzzi too. But how does he know I'm feeling the effects of yesterday? I thought I was hiding it quite well. I'm keen not to appear soft or feeble, though I'm not entirely sure why. I suppose because somewhere deep in my subconscious — where in my experience the most damage gets done — I have the notion that a fragile sub is not a lot of use to a tough Dom who enjoys his sport. A Dom like Daniel Riche. And I want to be of use, ergo, play down the aches and pains.

Dan's not fooled for a moment. He finishes his coffee and sticks a couple of slices of bread in the toaster. "Cornflakes or shredded wheat? I think my dear, health conscious brother might have some muesli in here somewhere…" He produces a bag of something strongly resembling birdseed from one of the cupboards, waggles it at me. I decline politely and select the cornflakes.

A bowl of cereals each, several slices of toast and two coffee refills later Dan heads off into the bathroom to fill the tub. I help myself to his racing paper and go to sit out on the rooftop decking beyond the picture windows. It's October, and getting chilly, but still pleasant enough to sit outside for a few minutes. I'm astonished to find two life-size models of sheep out there, grazing peacefully on Nathan Darke's fake grass. Quirky or what?

I leaf through the paper, not really that interested in racing statistics and form if I'm honest. I'm more taken with the view of Clarence Dock and the surrounding Leeds cityscape. Miles and miles of close packed rooftops, a lot of high rise buildings poking their heads up against the skyline, some open space, and as I raise my gaze to the farther horizons I can see the misty hills in the distance. Even here, the moors are in sight. I stay there, leaning on the parapet, wishing I had some binoculars and a map to pick out landmarks. Maybe another time…

I begin to shiver in the cool autumn morning so I head back inside. Dan is just emerging from the bathroom.

"There you are. Your bath's ready, madam."

"Why, thank you, Sir." I smile as I pass him, then gasp as I see the massive indoor swimming pool that passes for a bath in Nathan's apartment. It's made of wood, very dark wood, and looks deep enough to drown in. There are steps leading up the side. Open-mouthed, I go to peer over the rim. There's about three feet of steaming, scented water in there, coated with an enticing froth of bubbles. Seating is built in to the structure at various heights. It's quite wonderful. I turn to Dan, who is leaning in the doorway watching me explore. He's clearly amused.

"Anyone would think you'd never seen a bath before."

"I've never seen one like that. What's it made of?"

"I think Nathan said it was teak. Very warm. Drop the robe, Summer. Time to get in."

"Are you joining me?"

"Of course." He drops his sweatpants and, totally naked, strolls nonchalantly past me to bop up the steps and into the tub. He sinks into it, and lifts a hand to beckon me to join him.

It's just a gesture, not threatening exactly, but I feel a definite compulsion to obey and to do it fast. Not that I'm in the least reluctant—that water looks heavenly.

Moments later my robe is on the shiny black tiled floor along with Dan's pants, and I'm lowering myself into the bubbles. Dan stretches out an arm to help me negotiate the steps, then reaches out to flick the switch which activates the Jacuzzi jets. I lie back, my shoulders against Dan's chest and allow my feet to drift to the surface.

"This is lovely. Even better than at the club." I turn my head to smile up at him.

"Mmm, maybe you're just less tense. Less scared now?"

"Yes. I suppose." I think back to that night, my initiation into the world of kink. I *was* scared. I didn't trust Dan, or myself. I recognize now that I was looking for something different, some new way of being that was comfortable and safe and normal. At the same time I was terrified of change. I could feel the sands shifting under me that night, all my preconceived certainties wobbling perilously. I may have felt that my life was utter shite a lot of the time, but there's a lot to be said for the devil you know. The Summer Jones who ran scared from the Collared and Tied club and fled to Bristol would never have left a used condom on the bedroom floor all night.

I like today's Summer more, or I could get to like her. And I have Dan to thank for releasing her from wherever she was hiding. Was that all it took to beat the compulsions out of me? Six strokes with a belt and a butt plug up my arse?

Not quite that simple, I do realize. But I'm more relaxed, more confident in this moment than I remember feeling for a long, long time. Maybe forever.

"What's going on in that head of yours?" Dan's voice is quiet, little more than a soft murmur. He runs his hands up and down my arms, holding me safely so I have no need to worry about sinking. I trust him absolutely. But that doesn't mean I have ready answers for him. I don't fully understand myself so I can't explain to him what's different. Especially as he never really knew me before.

"No burning urge to fold up the towels or arrange the soap in color order."

Or didn't he?

"What do you mean?" I stiffen in his arms.

He hauls me back against his chest and this time lays his hands over my breasts, massaging the small mounds slowly. It's sensual, but oddly, not overtly sexual. More a caring, soothing gesture than one intended to arouse. Nevertheless, my pussy clenches. Dan's gentle, undemanding caress has the desired effect, though, and I'm soon drifting lazily, my body and mind now floating on the scented, swirling water.

"I noticed you lining up the coasters, that first night, in the bar. You were so uptight, like a spring about to snap. I think a spanking was just what you needed. You responded well to it."

"Yes." He's right. No point denying it. Or overanalyzing.

"And again yesterday. You tidied my bathroom cabinet. And that bag of yours—talk about military precision."

Ah, he did notice the bathroom then.

"If you hadn't been so obliging and earned those six strokes with my belt, I'd have had to spank you again any way. To loosen you up. So, was that good?"

I consider for a moment, then, "It was, Sir. Very good. I'd never imagined..." My voice trails away. I'm not sure what I'm trying to say. For once, Dan doesn't prompt me. He waits, patient. At last I find the words.

"I'd never imagined that hurting could feel good. Especially afterwards, but not just then. The pain was sort of, sort of cleansing, driving the shame away and making me into a clean sheet. And the things you said later, about moving on. I could. I really could. I did."

"I'm pleased. And can I say, sweet Summer Jones, while we're being so honest with each other that your submission last night totally blew me away. You were superb, a natural. My cock's twitching now just thinking about your gorgeous wet pussy after you'd accepted my belt, and you were even more wet and hot when the plug went in. I know you hated that, well at first you did anyway, maybe not so much by the time we'd finished. But you let me do it, my fingers first, then the plug. You just totally surrendered and let me do anything I wanted to you." He pauses, then, "Will you let me fuck your arse, Summer?"

No hesitation this time, my answer is instant, "Yes, Sir. Of course. I'd like that."

"Okay. So, we need to be back at Black Combe tomorrow, by one o'clock for the board meeting. Or I do. I assume you're not going back to Cumbria just yet?" He pauses.

I shake my head.

"Good. No other pressing engagements?"

Again I shake my head.

"No, Sir. None."

"That gives us the next twenty-four hours to enjoy each other, to explore your limits a bit more, maybe push them back further? Would you like that do you think? Would you stay here with me for the next twenty-four hours and turn your body over to me?"

"Will it hurt?" *Silly question.*

He chuckles. He obviously thinks it's a silly question too, but he answers anyway, "Oh yes. Some of the time. A lot of the time. But in a good way, like before. I intend to make you squeal. Will you squeal for me, little Summer of the three swallows?"

"I expect I will, Sir." I draw a deep breath, thinking about what it means to be hurting in a good way. My butt clenches instinctively but my response is certain. "Yes, Sir, I would like to stay here with you. And squeal."

"Excellent. First, though, we need more food. I suggest a Wetherspoon's brunch. You up for that?"

Now this I hadn't expected. I'd thought to find myself strapped to that cross in the bedroom before the last of the scented bubbles swirled down the plughole, so Dan's sudden change of tack is unnerving. But encouraging too. It's not all about the sex then. Not all about squealing. Not quite.

Chapter Four

In the end we decide against Wetherspoon's. Dan left me in the bath to enjoy a last soak on my own while he got dressed and finished his perusal of yesterday's racing news. By the time I eventually joined him in the living room he'd remembered a small, independent coffee shop in the ground floor of a mill conversion about ten minutes' walk away — one of Nathan's designs I gather — which he tells me does a fabulous Spanish omelet. Good enough for me. We descend in the lift, my face flaming as I recall vividly what happened in this same lift on our way up. Dan just smiles and pats my bottom.

"Later, sweetheart."

He winks at me, and I'm convinced my face is about to spontaneously combust. Who'd have imagined I could still feel embarrassed?

Who would imagine I could be embarrassed at all, particularly given the way I lost my virginity? Or rather, after I let my mother sell it.

I stumble slightly as we exit the large glass doors to the outside, and Dan catches my elbow to steady me. I study my feet as we walk, shocked at my sudden recollection. I usually manage to bury that memory, all those memories. I never think of that time, in Barrow, back at my mother's house. Well, almost never. It's banished as though it never happened. But there's something about being with Dan, some irresistible internal force that reawakens and resurrects those remembered images, forcing them back to the surface. Or would, if I let it.

I viciously suppress the recollection, and the sensations it evokes. I quash the shame and despair, as vivid now, today, as they were then. Even as I stroll along this dock in the pleasant autumn sunshine with a gorgeous man at my elbow, those feelings are as powerful as they were when I was sixteen. Back then I was just a defenseless pawn caught up in my mother's desperate games of survival. I tell myself it wasn't really her fault either, it was just how it was. For us, for her. Then. Not now, and not for me. I moved on. It's gone. It needs to stay gone.

"Are you alright? Not having second thoughts are you?" Dan sounds concerned.

I turn to look at him, puzzled.

"Something's upset you. You look really...distressed. Is it something I did?"

"No. *No!* I was just— It's nothing. Really."

"If you get scared, you've only to say. Your safe words are just that, they *will* keep you safe. And I'll push you, but never too far. You can trust me."

"I know." I stop, turn to face him. I need to make him understand that I do want this—this whatever it is we're doing. "I *do* know that. Really. I'm just being silly." On impulse I push up onto my toes and kiss his lips, the first time I've done so without being prompted.

If he's surprised he hides it well, enfolding me in his arms to deepen the kiss, his tongue spearing into my mouth to engage with mine. We snog like teenagers, oblivious to other Sunday morning strollers and anglers. Dan is first to break the kiss.

"My, my, Miss Jones. You do help me to work up an appetite, but delicious though you are I have my heart set on a cheese and ham toastie."

"What about the omelet?"

"A man's Sunday brunch is his own affair, Miss Jones. Now come on, before they run out of eggs."

* * * *

"Do you remember that night, when we met? The second time, I mean. In Lancaster."

"Vividly." He stirs his coffee slowly, his eyes on me. No doubt wondering where this is leading. I'm not entirely sure myself, but plow on regardless.

"The couples we saw. Watched. In the dungeon."

"Yes." He sips, regarding me over the rim of his cup. He offers no additional encouragement.

"I noticed that most of the women, well, all of them pretty much, seemed to have shaved their…" I know my face is flushing, though Christ only knows why. I really should be beyond embarrassment by now. My words fall away.

"Removed their pubic hair, yes. That's good grooming. Among submissives." Dan has to help me out after all. How kind.

"I see. Is it…common?"

"Yes, very. Most Dom's like it. Insist on it. Especially for their regular subs. It gives a whole new meaning to 'naked', sort of takes it up a notch."

"Do *you* like it?" I ask the question, but drop my gaze immediately. I'm getting into dangerous territory here. This could end badly, with me being hurt. Or humiliated. Or both. But it would appear my rampant curiosity knows no boundaries and my common sense was swilled down the plughole when I emptied the Jacuzzi.

"I do." His voice is soft, very quiet.

"Yet, you haven't asked me to shave myself." I'm muttering into my coffee now.

"Your hands are usually shaking so much, I'd be worried you might do irreparable damage."

His gentle humor is lost on me, sadly. I stare at my hands, and lo and behold they *are* shaking. I twist my fingers together in a vain attempt to restore order. Dan watches me for a few moments, then, "Look at me, Summer. Please."

I lift my gaze. His eyes are warm, that deep brandy richness glinting. My nervous stomach settles. Slightly. And my hands lie unmoving in my lap.

"And, you're not my regular sub."

He delivers the final killer line softly, and my stomach abandons its brief flirtation with anything resembling a settled state. *Oh God, why did I even start this?*

Suddenly a horrific thought strikes me. *Christ, what if...?*

"Do you have one? A regular sub, I mean?" I blurt out the question, staring at him, willing him to say no. This matters to me, really matters. I've no idea what I'll do if the answer is yes. It's rather late in the day to be raising this now, but it genuinely never occurred to me before.

Dan shakes his head, smiling kindly at me. And puts me out of my misery immediately. "No, Summer, I don't. Not at the moment." There's a brief pause before he smiles at me. "There's a vacancy, though, and I'm hoping you might consider the job."

"Me? You want *me*?" I can't keep the incredulous edge from my voice, my palm now splayed across the top of my chest to emphasize who we're talking about here. Me. Summer Jones. Skinny, uptight, plain and boring Summer Jones.

"Yes you."

"Me?" No harm in checking. Checking's good. "For more than just the twenty-four hours we said."

"You. And yes, more than just the twenty-four hours. I was intending to leave it until tomorrow before suggesting an extension. I thought I'd let you get used to my funny little ways a bit more, but since the issue has come up. Well?"

He looks amused now, leaning back in his chair to sip his coffee calmly while I continue to stare at him in disbelief.

"Would we have to go to the club again?" Again, I blurt out the first thing that pops into my head.

"The Collar? Yes, probably. Sometimes. Is that a problem?"

"It's just that I don't want to do things in public. I mean, when it's only you and me I feel... I mean it's..."

He reaches across the table and takes my hand, turning it palm up to caress it with his fingertips. "Nothing will happen that you don't want. I like to play in public from time to time, but I won't insist on it if it makes you unhappy."

"So, where then? I mean, I live with Freya in Kendal..." I'm not entirely sure of the relevance of that, but my brain is on overdrive, hurling random thoughts around. I'm working hard to see how this would play out between us. As usual, I'm locked on to the details when it's the major principles I should be considering. Will I or won't I? Can I? Should I? I know that Dan works at the zoo in Cumbria and at Cartmel racecourse, so maybe he does live somewhere near to me. Always it's the practicalities I hone in on.

Dan chuckles. "Well, I suspect you'll be living alone now. Freya's moved in with Nick."

"Yes, she told me. But even so…"

Dan squeezes my hand still lying between his palms. "Just say yes, love, and let me work out the kinks. Pun intended."

I gaze at him, and the silence stretches between us. He tilts his head, questioning, wondering. Hoping? And it's that that settles it for me.

"Yes. Yes please, Sir. I'd like that. I think."

"I think so too. I know I will. So, about your pubic hair…?"

"My…?"

"Well you started this. I prefer it waxed rather than shaved though. Less bristles that way."

"I've never… I mean, I don't know how to…" I cross my legs instinctively. *Waxing? There? Ouch.*

"It *is* possible to do a Brazilian wax yourself, but I think the first time it would be better to have it done professionally. That said, Nathan's quite good at it."

"No! I mean, you wouldn't…" It occurs to me he could insist, and I'd have to obey him. I've learned enough already to understand that's how this works. *Oh God, what have I done?*

"No, I wouldn't. I doubt if he would either. Eva'd have his nuts in a vice if he so much as considered it. No, I suggest you ask Freya where she goes and book an appointment."

Thank God for that. "I see. Right, I will. Next week, when I'm back in Kendal."

"Good. So, little subbie, have you finished your coffee? Ready to go back to Nathan's apartment and experiment a little more?"

I nod, pushing my empty cup away. We stroll back out into the crisp morning. Dan takes my hand as we make our unhurried way along Clarence Dock.

"Will you tie me to the cross? The one in the bedroom?" *Now where did that come from?*

He glances at me, one eyebrow raised. "Would you like that?"

I nod, hoping he'll settle for that and not press me to elaborate. No such luck.

"Front or back?"

"What do you mean?"

"I mean, do you want me to whip your front, your breasts, your clit, or your back. I prefer the front, but that can be a little intense. And you are just a beginner…"

I glance up, startled, my head again spinning as the vivid imagery unfurls. He winks at me, his expression amused, wicked, lustful. Despite my nervousness, I grin back. My pussy is moistening already. This 'regular sub' business could really turn out to be rather nice.

* * * *

"Is that comfortable? Not too tight?"

"I'm fine. I think." I tug experimentally on the leather restraints securing my wrists to the two upper extremes of the St Andrew's Cross. No give there. Dan crouches beside me to tighten the straps around my ankles. My legs are spread wide, the intent obvious. A good sign, I'm minded to think.

Dan ordered me to strip as soon as we arrived back at the apartment. I complied, naturally. I was equally acquiescent when he instructed me to lean on the cross, facing it, and position myself in the restraints. Satisfied now that I am in place and ready, Dan pats me on the bum before turning away to open the chest at the foot of the bed. Craning my neck to see, I watch as he leans in to pick something up. He straightens, and I see he's selected a suede flogger. It's made up of a bunch of separate strands, each one tipped with a small bead. They click ominously against each other as he returns to my side, the flogger dangling from his hand.

"Do you want me to tell you what's going to happen? Or would you prefer me to just get on with it? In the future I'm not likely to offer you a choice, but I'm making allowances right now, in view of your inexperience."

How generous. I consider my options for a few moments. "Just do it please."

"Good choice. I will want to talk to you after, though. Now, I'm going to blindfold you."

It's a statement rather than a question. He's not asking permission, but even so I have just enough time to nod my agreement before he slips the blindfold over my eyes and my world goes black.

"Safe words. Are they still red, amber and green?" He's close up behind me, his breath brushing my neck as he talks to me.

"Yes, Sir."

"Fine. Use them if you need to. Especially don't hesitate to use amber. I'll be happy to slow down, or explain. This is meant to be edgy, you're meant to squirm a bit. But if you get scared, or it's too intense for you, I want to know. Got that?"

"Yes, Sir."

"God, I like you, Summer. You and your pretty little swallows." I jump as he touches my bottom with, I think, the handle of the flogger. It feels hard, cool. He trails it up the edge of my right buttock, across my tattoos. "You still have faint stripes from yesterday. Very pretty, but I think we'll avoid them today. I want your skin to heal properly before I spank you again.

"That's very kind of you, Sir. Very considerate."

"I'll tolerate a little sarcasm from my subs, but not too much. You're at your limit now, Summer. Remember that before you let your cheeky mouth get you in bother."

I detect the subtle shift in his tone, a cool hardness. His Dom voice. I know when to keep a low profile — learned that a long time ago.

"I apologize, Sir. It won't happen again." I drop my head, slumping in my restraints. He said he'd just get on with it, yet here we are, still talking. Every time I open my mouth I seem to stick my foot in it. And he scares me far more with his words than with his whip.

"Summer? You seem unhappy suddenly. Is something wrong?"

"No, Sir. Please, I'm fine."

"Don't lie to me. You're not fine and I want to know why." His tone is harder now, all Dom, all demanding. Stern and intolerant. He believes I'm lying to him, or deliberately evading his questions and either is unacceptable. Either will earn me a punishment.

The situation is spiraling away from me and my heart continues to sink. How has this happened? Where did my easy confidence of a few moments ago disappear to? In the face of his implacable insistence I have no choice but to attempt to explain.

"You're angry, and that scares me. I want to please you, but I seem to irritate you without intending to." I can hear the catch in my voice, the wavering that usually precedes tears. I don't want to cry, not again, not now.

He says nothing, appears to be waiting for me to finish. I can't see him, but I feel his breath on my neck. I consciously raise my chin and stiffen my shoulders before continuing, "I don't feel to be in control..."

"You're not in control. I am."

"But of me, of what I feel, what I do..."

"You handed control to me. All of it. You can get it back with your safe words, but until you do, unless you do, I'm running this show and you just accept it. Take it. Don't try to fight me, you've no need to. I'll hurt you, because that's what you need from me, some of the time at least, but I won't harm you. Ever. You *can* trust me."

His fingers are on my shoulders, both his hands so he must have put the flogger down. He massages my shoulders firmly. "Relax, Summer. Just relax and let yourself feel. Just be, and stop fretting."

I roll my head, my neck muscles stretching and releasing, and with that the crippling tension of a few minutes ago dissipates. My body loosens and melts under his probing, demanding caress, as though he's drawing all my pent-up anxieties out through his fingers. He keeps up the motion for a few minutes, working his way down my spine to my buttocks. He slips one hand between my legs, probing through my wet folds to rub my clit before plunging two fingers inside me.

"I think you're enjoying yourself a little more now, Summer. Am I right?"

"Yes, Sir." My voice is a hushed murmur, but all trace of distress is gone. "That feels so good, Sir."

"Hot and tight. Your perfect little pussy, just waiting to be fucked. Am I right about that too?"

"You are, Sir."

He withdraws his fingers, and I moan slightly as he steps away, the intimate, soothing contact broken.

"All in good time. First, I have plans for you. Ten strokes I think. I'll count, you concentrate on breathing. Breathe in before each stroke, and out afterwards. Clear?"

"Yes, Sir. I'll try."

"Summer?" Trying isn't enough this time.

"Yes, Sir, perfectly clear. I'm ready."

There's a slight rustle of clothing, and I assume he's bent to retrieve the flogger. It's to be now then. The talking's over at last. I remember my instructions and draw in a deep breath, wondering how long I'll have to hold it for. Not long at all. A breath of air, just the merest whisper as the suede strands fly. I gasp as they connect with the tender skin across my shoulder blades. The beads sting, each one its own pinprick of pain, sharp and vivid but not too intense. I arch instinctively, but don't cry out.

"One. Breathe out now, Summer."

I do, releasing the air trapped in my lungs. Dan waits patiently while I refill them. The air shifts and whistles again as Dan aims the flogger, this time at a spot just below my shoulder blades. The sharp bite of the beads causes me to wince, but the strands themselves are gentle, soft on my skin. I hadn't expected that. I sigh as I exhale, sagging into the large

V space between the arms of the cross, relying on just the restraints to hold me up.

"Two."

I breathe in, and hold, waiting for the swish of the flogger. Dan lays the strands across my lower back this time, slightly harder than before. I do cry out, but softly. He hasn't hurt me, yet. Soon.

"Three."

I let out my breath, draw in the next in calm anticipation.

"Four. Five. Six."

I'm settled, comfortable in my rhythm. Dan's increasing the intensity, but only marginally, maybe. I'm not entirely sure.

"Seven."

I squeal, now I am sure. That was hard. That hurt.

"Just wanted to make sure you were still awake."

"Thank you, Sir."

"Was that more sarcasm, Summer?" His tone is deceptively mild.

"No, Sir. I'm sorry."

"Breathe in again, girl."

I do, and scream as the next stroke lands across my shoulders, the pain now sharp and burning as he flogs my tender, sensitized skin. I'm gasping, my body tensing, listening for the telltale whoosh that signals the next stroke.

I hear it the merest moment before the pain explodes across my back.

"Eight. The last two will be harder still. Ready?"

I nod, unable to get any words out just in this moment. My skin is smarting and burning, each tiny point where the beads have struck me now tingling and throbbing. *Two left? Only two? I can do this. I want this.*

The air shifts again as the flogger whistles its descent. I jerk, my head flying back. My eyes are wide open as I stare at the ceiling, but I don't scream. That was harder, but the pain was less. I feel strangely welcoming of the next and final blow, wishing it wasn't the last. Just as I'm beginning to love the sharp intensity of the beads striking my back and shoulders, to crave it, he's about to stop.

"More please." Is that my voice, my breathy whisper?

"One more, then we stop. With the flogger at least. I have lots more planned for you, though, greedy little sub. Breathe." His voice is all Dom, stern and unrelenting. There will be no extending this experience, no point asking again.

Obedient, I draw in a long, deep breath. The final stroke is excruciating. And wondrous, and uplifting. Liberating. I scream, but whether in pain or mindless joy I have no idea. I'm aware only of pure sensation, clean, sharp white-hot pain, an agony of pleasure.

I'm hanging on the cross, my body suspended between pain and something else, something only now starting to unfurl. Something deeply satisfying, cleansing, almost spiritual. Even as I'm trying to process what's happening, what I'm feeling, I sigh as Dan slides his fingers between my wide-spread legs. He strokes my slick, hot pussy tenderly. My wetness is smeared across his fingertips, and he spreads it everywhere. He slides upwards, backwards, between my buttocks to my arsehole. Without uttering a word he slips the tip of his finger inside, working the hole as he did yesterday. My resistance is non-existent, and in moments his entire finger is deep inside my arse.

"Good girl. Now two."

I nod, though my consent is obvious. I'm groaning my pleasure, my delight at his gentle but insistent probing, and soon my arse is stretched to accommodate two fingers. He thrusts, and twists his hand to work me even looser before easing a third finger in. Now it's hard, really difficult. I moan, he's hurting me. He knows it, and his movements are slow, giving me time to adjust and to accept. I don't ask him to stop. I want this. I know where this is leading, and I want all of it.

The discomfort recedes as my arsehole relaxes, the muscles there loosening to accommodate Dan's fingers. He leans in close to me, his body resting against my smarting, inflamed back as he reaches around me to caress my clit. It's enough, more than enough. I orgasm instantly, shaking and quivering in the restraints as my body convulses. Dan thrusts his fingers deep, my arse now totally conquered and accepting the intrusion. He finger fucks me hard and sharp, and I'm astonished at how sweet it feels, how erotic. Intimate, profoundly personal, his connection to me emphasized, his possession assured, every other sensation intensified by the deep and unfamiliar penetration.

My orgasm seems to go on and on, wave after wave of sensual pleasure thrumming through my veins. I shift, seeking more friction, harder, faster, deeper. Dan delivers, and my release soars again, shaking my core and blossoming through my outstretched arms and legs. Even my fingers and toes are tingling with pure delight. It's carnal, animalistic almost. And the most intensely satisfying experience I have ever encountered. Sex with Dan has always been good, always left me purring, but this is on a different plane. Now, I'm flying.

At last, at long last, the sensations fade, start to recede. I'm dimly aware that he's withdrawn his fingers and is unfastening my restraints. His arm around my waist prevents me from collapsing in a heap at his feet. He bends to release my ankles, then lifts me. He places me on the bed, rolling me over onto my stomach. A sharp pat on my bum tells me to stay there. I'm going nowhere in any case.

The sound of running water from the en suite tells me that Dan's attention to hygiene is very much to the fore, and I'm grateful for it. He cares, takes responsibility for me. I'm beginning to understand why. This power transfer he talks about means he's accountable. And I can simply abandon myself to him. I do. I have.

Moments later he's back. I turn my head, watch him quickly undress. His cock is huge, his erection solid and thick, and proudly pointing straight up. I'm eying it appreciatively as Dan snaps the foil on a condom and unrolls it along his length. Next he takes a tube of lubricant from the bedside table and quickly squeezes a generous blob into his palm. He smears it over the length of his cock, coating the smooth latex before coming to kneel on the bed alongside me.

"I want you on your hands and knees, legs spread wide."

I say nothing, just bend my knees to push myself up from the duvet.

"If it's more comfortable you can drop your shoulders down, as long as your bum's in the air for me. Arch your back as I've taught you. Present your arse, girl." Again, that stern, uncompromising Dom tone. But without menace.

He knows what he's doing. I trust him. His intent is obvious, and I have no hesitation in doing as he says.

I'm beyond embarrassment. Humiliation is just a memory. I trust him to take care of me. As I lower my shoulders to the bed and lay my cheek against the pillow he takes the tube again and helps himself to another large dollop.

"You're already wet, but this is your first time. I intend to take good care of your sweet little virgin arse." He spreads the slick, cool gel around my now loose and welcoming arsehole, then works it inside. Two fingers, then the third. It's not painful this time, just pleasantly tight. I gyrate my hips in enthusiastic contentment.

"Entering into the spirit. That's what we like to see." He pulls his fingers from my arse and moves to kneel behind me. "I'm going to go slow, and I'll stop and wait whenever you need me to. You have your safe words. There's no hurry. But I *am* going to be inside you. All, the way. You *can* take all of me, and you will. Is that clear?"

"Yes, Sir." If he says so, though I already know he's huge. This is not going to be easy. Despite all my good intentions I start to tense up.

He knows straight away, his palms caressing my buttocks.

"Trust me, love." His words are soft, his fingers tracing the edge of my arsehole, teasing, arousing. Tantalizing.

My body relaxes again, and he places the head of his cock inside my arse. Just the head, no more, the sphincter stretched tight around it. Three fingers felt large, this is more. Much more. He pushes forward, slow and smooth. Inch by careful inch he enters me.

It hurts, and I'm scared. My fingers are like claws, grasping at the pillow beneath my head. I'm gnawing on my lower lip as he pushes again, my arse opening wide to accept his unrelenting entry. He stops, slides his fingertips through the slick lube coating the delicate, sensitive skin around my anus, circling the shaft of his cock now embedded deep but not fully inside me. Despite my nervousness and my discomfort it does feel good. Sort of. His touch is soothing and reassuring, his concentration focused on me.

The pressure starts again, his cock slips deeper in. And deeper still. I'm whimpering, whether in fear or pain I'm not certain, but it never occurs to me to say amber. He's going slow, as he promised he would, allowing me ample time to respond. I do, by raising my bum a little higher, welcoming him, urging him on. His palm against my buttock is his acknowledgment, a gentle caress as he stretches his thumb to reach between my folds to dip the tip of it in my wet pussy. It's the reminder I need of how aroused I am, of the exciting intensity I'm discovering on this voyage of sensual discovery.

My whimpers become moans of pleasure as he reaches around me with his other hand to place the pad of his middle finger over my clit.

"Will this help, little slut?"

I nod in near desperation. "Yes, Sir. Please. Now, please..."

He presses and rubs, at the same time somehow manipulating his thumb to hit my G-spot. I melt into an orgasmic haze as he slides his cock fully home, no longer tense, any vestige of lingering, subconscious resistance gone.

He doesn't thrust, doesn't move inside me at all. Just remains there, continuing to use his fingers to caress me until I stop coming. Although he's unmoving, my arse is clenching around him, tighter with each delightful wave of ecstasy. I'm full, more than I could ever have imagined and stretched to my limit, but it's fine. I'm fine, as he said I would be. As the tingles of my release ebb away they're replaced by a wave of intense gratitude. He kept his word. I trusted him, and he's taking care of me.

"Summer?" His voice is low and soft, a warm, rich murmur, seeking confirmation that I'm alright.

I don't think I could manage to speak at this moment, my emotions are much too close to the surface. Instead I stretch out my hand to close around his, now resting on the duvet on either side of my shoulders. I squeeze. It seems to be enough, because he leans in to kiss that sensitive spot between my shoulder blades, still warm from the flogging.

"That's all of me. You've done well. Am I hurting you?"

I shake my head.

"Good. I'll be gentle, and I want you to tell me if I *do* hurt you. Yes?"

Again, I can't manage words, but I nod. He starts to move. Slow at first, he withdraws his cock maybe halfway before sliding it back in again. He waits a moment before doing it again. And once more. I groan, my fingers opening and closing around handfuls of duvet. Dan stops.

"Summer, is this too hard, too fast?"

"No, I'm fine. I am, really. It just feels so, so…"

He chuckles. "I get the picture. And did I mention, little slut, how very beautiful you are?"

"No, Sir. Not that I can recall."

He gives the side of my bum a playful tap. "Liar. Now stop distracting me. I'm trying to concentrate here."

"My apologies, Sir. And I would appreciate it if you could manage to pay attention." *Who knew I could find it in me to be flippant at a time like this?*

Chuckling, he withdraws again, almost pulling right out before he plunges back in, deep and harder now. The sensation is intense, a sweet, ragged friction deep inside, intimate, decadent. Wicked and forbidden and quite, quite breathtaking. A tightness starts to form low down in my body, another orgasm starting to unfurl. My hands form tight, desperate fists as the pleasure grows and warms. My pussy quivers deliciously, and I wish longingly for him to finger fuck me too. That would be so good, so...

"Oh Christ. Sir, I..." My voice trails off as he picks up a rhythm, solid, certain. Deep and penetrating, searching for my response. I give, it. I have no choice, it bursts from me as my body spasms uncontrollably.

Dan leans forward, slips his hands beneath my shoulders and hauls me upright, onto his thighs. I lean back against his chest as he arranges my knees on the outer sides of his own and spreads my legs wide.

"Look." He whispers the single word into my ear, pointing to the mirror strategically fixed to a wardrobe across the room. I open my eyes and stare transfixed at my image, our image, reflected there. My body is pale in comparison to Dan's healthy tanned glow, his shoulders visible above and behind me, his legs under mine. But the rest of the tableau is me, just me in nude, aroused glory, my nipples deeply pink and swollen. My stomach is gently rounded, the triangle of pale hair beneath blending subtly with my own creamy skin tones. As I watch Dan lowers his hand to stroke my wispy curls.

"This is lovely, like you, but it has to go. Agreed?"

"Yes." My answer is a breathy moan as my pussy squeezes and clenches again, desperate to be filled. Dan reaches around to caress my left breast, his right hand sliding between my glistening folds.

"If you were waxed, truly naked for me, we'd be able to see your sweet little clit. Just here, see?" He parts my folds with his fingers to expose the sensitive nub. "So swollen, so hot. Is it throbbing, my gorgeous little slut?"

"Yes, Sir," I whisper.

"Mmm, thought it might be."

He draws his fingertip slowly along the length of my clit, lightly, barely touching me although it feels like every single nerve ending is reaching out, quivering for him. My mouth is open—I'm panting now, my arousal nearing desperate, explosive proportions.

"Please don't tease me, Sir. Not now."

"I guess you're right. Is this better." He leans around me to reach just a little more, sufficient to plunge three fingers upwards into my hot, spasming cunt.

I scream, thrusting my hips forward. He keeps the heel of his hand firmly against my clit as I rub myself frantically against him, the muscles in my pussy gripping his fingers. My arse is clenching too, hard and tight like a fist around his solid length. I'm writhing and gyrating like a wild thing, but Dan's arms and hands remain locked around me, in me, keeping me in place and never letting up until every last quiver and tingle of this latest orgasm is wrung from me. Throughout, Dan's voice is in my ear, his words soothing and reassuring through the storm of pure sensation which would have been close to overwhelming without him to anchor me.

"Enjoy, love. Let it go. I have you." I hear him, responding to the soft, safe murmur, emotionally and physically.

He has me. He truly does. And now, I have him. In that moment I know, I'm never letting go.

Chapter Five

"Stick your arm out, I want to test something on you."

"What?" I glance up from the magazine I am reading, my legs tucked up underneath me on the leather sofa in the living room. My stomach is pleasantly full, courtesy of a selection of delicious Asian tapas-style dishes Dan had sent up from the Kashmiri restaurant and buffet down in the shopping plaza of Clarence Dock. We both agreed we had no wish at all to go to all the bother of getting dressed and eating out, but we were hungry and couldn't find inspiration in Nathan's freezer. So Dan phoned the restaurant and asked them to prepare a selection, which arrived beautifully arrayed on a tray made up of separate segmented disposable dishes. We set it up on the low table in the lounge and had a carpet picnic, washed down with sparkling water from Nathan's fridge dispenser.

I'm wearing just my knickers and a loose shirt, unbuttoned. Dan would have been wearing even less than me but it occurred to him he might spill chili sauce, which could prove unsettling to say the least. Also, he didn't want to give the young man who delivered our meal any cause to have us struck off their rounds. A decent curry is something of a rarity in Leeds, he tells me seriously. We need to look after this supplier, being so handy as well.

Our meal finished, Dan cleared away the empties, which mostly amounted to piling the whole lot into the waste disposal chute, and set about brewing some coffee. I found a copy of Yorkshire Life in a drawer under the table so I'd been amusing myself leafing through the pictures of manicured terraced gardens and picturesque rural retreats, ponies and croquet lawns, the haunts and pastimes of the county's elite. Which I suppose probably includes Nathan Darke, though Dan has not struck me as remotely interested in the trappings of wealth. Come to think of it, he and Freya would get on well.

I turn to Dan, wondering what he might have in mind now. He's already making his way over to me. He has a small porcelain dish in his palm, which he places on the low table beside the sofa.

"Your arm, please. I need to do a patch test."

"A what?" I'm not sure where this is going, but I have no hesitation in rolling back my long sleeve to present my arm. Dan perches on the edge of the sofa, my elbow across his lap. He dips his finger in the little dish, then daubs whatever it is on the soft skin of my inner arm. I look at it closely. It's a colorless liquid, oily. As I lean over I catch a whiff of peppermint.

"What is that?"

"Peppermint oil. I want to check that you're not allergic to it. And get the right dilution for you. Too weak and you'll miss out on the fizz. Too strong and—well, we just don't want it too strong, that's all.

If your arm hasn't swollen and turned black in the next half hour we'll do another test somewhere more sensitive. Your lips perhaps."

He leans down to kiss me. I curl my arm around his neck to deepen the kiss when he would have broken it. Entering into the spirit of things and reaching blindly to replace the dish on the table, Dan rolls onto the sofa with me, and soon we're tangling limbs and tongues, trading sensual caresses.

In no time my shirt is on the floor, Dan's sweatpants too. I reach for his cock, erect and solid in my hand. I tighten my grip around him, pumping gently. This is the first time I've initiated sex with Dan, and it's a heady experience. I feel powerful, demanding. In control, but not fraught with the usual tension I associate with being responsible. I'm not consumed by a need to steer and keep order, to regulate or contain. I can just be, I can simply enjoy.

Dan rolls onto his back, his hands folded behind his neck. His eyes are closed. I slip from the sofa to kneel on the floor beside him, both my hands wrapped around the shaft of his cock. I take a moment to study it, the round, deep pink head, already glistening with the slick liquid seeping from the slit at the end. I rub the pad of my thumb through it, smearing it all over. His cock jerks in my hand, which I take to be a sign of approval. I do it again, with a similar result. Dan's eyes remain closed, his expression serene but his lips quirk sexily. He says nothing, but I know. Just as he knows his effect on me, I'm reading his signals.

I lean over, angling his cock toward me with my hands and holding it steady while I draw the tip of my tongue around the swollen, solid head. The liquid there tastes salty. It's pleasant, delicious even. I return for more, lapping greedily. The savory flavor increases, as more liquid emerges. I run my tongue around the groove where the shaft joins the head, and note that he jerks when I lick the underside. *Yes!*

I do it again. And again, pumping slowly with both hands. Dan groans, one arm now flung across his forehead. I speed up, and lean over him to take the entire head of his cock in my mouth. I suck, hollowing my cheeks around him and rubbing the underside of his cock with my tongue. His other hand is now in my hair, tangling it, gripping a fistful. He holds my head still for a moment, thrusting his hips to push his cock toward the back of my throat. I gag, unused to this, and he releases my hair instantly. His hips are still, but knowing what he wants I take over, my head now bobbing rhythmically as I continue to run my hand up and down the shaft. With my other hand I reach between his legs for his balls. I squeeze them experimentally, much less certain of my reception here. James always said I was too rough…

Dan is seemingly made of sterner stuff. His muttered "Christ, yes. Holy fuck!" seems pretty conclusive to me, and I roll the solid orbs firmly, loving the way they seem to shift and move in their sac. I curl my fingers to run my nails over his scrotum, which also seems to go down well. His legs part to allow me better access, so I slide my hand farther still, along his perineum, right to his arsehole. Two can play these games, perhaps. And often do.

I circle his anus with my finger, wondering what he'd do if I…

"You'll need lube. In the bedside drawer."

I need no more encouragement. With a whispered instruction not to move, I leap up and run across the room. I grab the tube from the drawer then sprint back, squirting it onto my finger as I go. In moments

I'm back where I was, sucking greedily on his cock, sliding my fist up and sown the shaft, and testing his arsehole with one well slicked finger.

I meet nothing that could be even remotely described as resistance. Has he done this before? He must have. He likes it, he knew he would. I'm careful even so. He might know what he's doing but I don't. I'm glad I have fairly short nails, and he probably is too. I apply a slight pressure, my finger goes deeper. I press again, and sink a little deeper in. Dan groans, louder this time, lifting his hips, pressing against my hand. He wants more. I twist my hand slightly and push harder. The rest of my finger slips in.

I have to check, must ask. "Is this okay, Sir?"

"Fucking perfect." His reply is succinct, but leaves no room for doubt.

I withdraw my finger halfway then plunge it back. He grimace speaks of pleasure, appreciation and a growing satisfaction. My confidence is building fast, I don't feel a need to watch his face so intently now. My attention is back on his magnificent cock which is jerking furiously in my mouth. I suck it, lick it, flick it with my tongue, graze it with my teeth. All of this is punctuated by moans of male delight and approval. I thrust my finger in and out of his arse, consider adding a second one but decide not to push my luck. I'll ask him about that. Later. For now, I'm intent on bringing him to a climax. I owe him so many, though I doubt either of us has kept count.

My head and shoulders are moving evenly, my rhythm smooth and in time with the actions of my hands. I bring my fist up the shaft as my head goes down, and pull back down toward the base as I lift up, I maintain the suction, using my tongue and teeth to tease the wide, smooth head. I'm rewarded by spurts of more salty liquid, and Dan's hips thrust violently upwards. My finger in his arse is plunging deep, each stroke eliciting a groan of sheer pleasure.

Dan's climax is building fast, and I wonder if I should slow down, try to prolong this. As though linked telepathically he mutters to me not to stop. "Christ, Summer... For fuck's sake—harder. More, girl."

I do as he asked, finding an extra gear for my aching wrists and stiffening shoulders. With a hoarse shout he comes, his semen bursting from his cock and filling my mouth. I swallow, fast, clear my airway, never letting up the pressure. The semen continues to flow, splashing across my tongue to be swallowed hungrily. Only when the eruption finally slows and his frantic jerking ceases do I allow myself to slow down.

I pull my finger slowly from his arse, lift my head to release his cock. He looks exhausted, and I feel drained too. I've never done anything like that before, hadn't known my power to affect him. This is heady stuff. Still holding his cock in my hand, but loosely now, I lay my forehead on his stomach. He reaches for me, his fingers again in my hair, stroking and combing. I turn my head to look at him, my cheek now pressed against his chest. I can hear his heartbeat, rapid but slowing, vigorous, healthy. Totally alive.

"Fuck me, Summer. You learn fast." He hasn't opened his eyes. His voice is low, sexy, warm.

I lay a kiss on his flat nipple before answering, "Thank you, Sir. Would you like me to fuck you now, or would you prefer to wait for a short while?" I caress his softening cock, schooling my features so as not to smile, even though he's not actually looking at me. You never know.

"Have a care, girl. I have a near uncontrollable urge to spank you. Can't think what's causing it. Go and wash your hands while I consider the matter."

There, I knew it.

"Would that be a punishment spanking, Sir?" I try for a guileless tone, but may not succeed, as I scramble to my feet. I stroll across to the kitchen area and rinse my hands under the warm tap, squeezing a blob of washing-up liquid into my palm for good measure.

"That's not my plan just at the moment, but carry on with the attitude and it will be."

I glance over my shoulder as I dry my hands to see that his eyes are still closed. He pauses, his expression now thoughtful, even though he has yet to prise open his eyelids. Then, "Oh fuck, just the thought of spanking you has set me off. Get back over here. Fast."

He sits up suddenly, swinging around to put his feet on the floor. I know better than to hang about, I'm back by his side in a moment.

"Assume the position, girl." He pats his knee, his gaze warm but stern.

His Dom attitude is emerging fast, and my inner submissive is suitably impressed. My pussy is clenching, moistening as I drop down to kneel at his feet. I look up at him, his beautiful dark brown eyes hot and sexy and absolutely uncompromising. This is happening, and it's going to be good. Not punishment he said. So that leaves…

"Summer, do *not* keep me waiting."

"No, Sir." *As if.*

I clamber across his lap to arrange myself face down. I'm still wearing my knickers, now very damp. Dan hooks his finger under the elastic waistband, twangs it hard.

"Take these off please."

"Yes, Sir." I reach back, pull my pants down and past my knees, then kick them away. I settle back across his lap, my bum conveniently bared and raised for whatever he decides to do.

"Five slaps, then you open your legs to let me test how wet you are. You count, and spread 'em wide after five. Understood?"

I barely have the chance to confirm my agreement before the first spank lands, sharp and stinging on my left buttock. It makes me squeal, but I couldn't truly say he hurt me. I brace, waiting for the next one.

"I told you to count." His tone is firm and cool, though his hand is anything but as he palms my smarting bum.

"Sorry, Sir. That's one."

He slaps me again, on the right side this time.

"Two, Sir. Three. Four."

The slaps fall, evenly spaced across my bottom. Hard enough to sting, but not really painful. This is arousal, pure and simple and deadly in its effectiveness. My pussy is squeezing frantically, I'm conscious of the gathering wetness. One more spank and I can spread my legs for him to touch me.

"Five, Sir." I part my thighs as wide as I can in this position.

Dan shifts, raising one knee to lift my bum higher and leans around to part my folds with his fingers.

"You look wet. All shiny and pink, like a cherry. I'd say you look juicy. Do you feel juicy, Summer?"

"I'm not sure, Sir. I'll be guided by you."

"Good answer. Get up."

"What? Why, Sir? I thought..." I'm confused, and disappointed. Just as things were getting good it seems he's done with me. I tumble to the floor, turning to stare up at him rebelliously.

He chuckles, amused by my obvious frustration. "An argumentative little slut. How nice. We are going to have some fun. You can take that horrified look off your face and go grab some toys from the bedroom. In the chest at the foot of the bed you'll find a vibrator. Several actually. Choose one. And some Ben Wa balls. Do you know what those look like?"

I shake my head slowly, my head spinning with possibilities. He had me as soon as he mentioned the vibrator.

"Silver metal, two balls, about this size" — he makes a circle of his thumb and index finger to illustrate — "fastened together on a silicone cord. Bring those too please." He pauses again. "Whenever you're ready...?"

I leap to my feet and rush across the room, back into the bedroom. I throw open the chest lid, and kneel beside it to survey the contents. Even though I knew what to expect, the array of toys, equipment, implements, whatever he might choose to call this stuff, is dizzying. I stare for a moment, briefly stunned at the prospect of sampling even a small selection of this treasure trove. I smile to myself, conscious of how quickly my perception has shifted. With trust comes, well, everything really.

"Summer? Today if you don't mind." Dan's voice is stern, the words clipped. No time to daydream here.

"Sorry, Sir. I won't be a moment." I reach in and grab a pale orange dildo. It has a switch on the base which I flick to test. The thing starts to whir and shake in my hand. I decide it seems fine. Rather nice in fact.

I glance down into the bowels of the chest again, and the glint of the metallic balls catches my eye. I grab those too and close the lid. Carrying my new playthings I return to Dan in the next room. He has the tube of lubricant in his hand, and he passes that to me in exchange for the balls.

"Lube up the dildo, then I want you back across my lap. Legs open, naturally."

Naturally. I waste no time in smearing the slick goo across the head and shaft of the dildo. I hand it back to him before returning to my original position, my bottom helpfully raised for further inspection. Dan does not keep me waiting.

His fingers are cool as they slide into my pussy. He thrusts hard. I grasp his ankle as a wave of undiluted pleasure starts deep in my cunt, rippling outwards. I shiver, tightening my inner muscles around his fingers as he rubs my G-spot.

"You seem eager, Miss Jones. Shall we see how you like this then?"

He pulls his fingers out and shifts his position again, twisting to be able to view my pussy. He gently parts the lips with his fingers and slips the head of the dildo between them. "This might feel a little cool, but it'll soon warm up. You okay, Summer?"

"Yes, Sir. I'm fine."

He presses gently and the dildo slides easily into me. Even this time yesterday I would have been mortified with embarrassment at the way he's handling my body, and at my helpless response to him. But not today, not now. I lie still, loving the feel of his hands on my skin, still smarting slightly from the spanking earlier, his palms now caressing my bum, stroking my pretty swallows before he flicks the switch on the base of the vibrator and the delightful undulations start. The sensations flow along the length of my channel, wicked and exquisite, and deeply sensual. I gasp, grab his ankle again.

"Oh, Sir…"

"Nice?"

"Yes, Sir. Very nice."

He reaches around and under me to take my clit between his thumb and index finger. He squeezes, rolls it gently, then more firmly.

"Nicer?" His words are spoken low, his voice rich and sexy.

I can only nod my response and tighten my grip around his ankle. Dan understands, though, and increases the pressure. I'm writhing on his lap, instinctively rubbing my throbbing nub against his hand, desperate for more friction, more sensation, more everything. Dan provides it, all of it and more. In moments I'm hurtling toward orgasm.

"Come for me, Summer. Now. Come hard." He encourages me, urging me on as he rubs my clit. The pressure intensifies as the vibrator continues to throb and pulse inside me.

I'm grasping for my climax, just out of reach, still eluding me. With a knowing chuckle Dan slides his finger around my pussy, picking up any surplus lube to oil his finger. Before I realize what he intends he's slipping his finger into my arse, sliding deep. The double penetration is intense, powerful, fiercely wicked. I climax wildly, instantly, screaming in pleasure as my body splinters. I swear I can see lights flashing behind my eyes, can hear a roaring in my ears, but otherwise I'm oblivious to everything apart from the unyielding, mindless delight of this moment.

My climax is over, almost as quickly as it began, but Dan is nowhere near done it seems. He pulls his finger from my arse, at the same time using his other hand to switch off the vibrator and slide that out too. I'm still spasming pleasantly when he slips the first of the Ben Wa balls into my pussy.

"What... What's that, Sir?"

"Questions later. For now, safe word or keep quiet."

Well, I won't be using my safe word any time soon. I close my mouth, concentrate on what he's doing now. The other ball soon follows the first, and Dan taps my bum smartly. "Close your legs, Summer. Time to finish your spanking. I think another twenty slaps, don't you? I want you to count, and when I tell you to, you'll open your legs wide for me to slap your pussy too. Got that?"

"Yes, Sir." I have no hesitation. He's trained me well. And so quickly.

The first spank lands, hard and sharp. The balls inside me shudder, rolling against my sensitive pussy walls, the weights inside them shifting. The feeling is quite fabulous, gentle yet deeply satisfying. I hadn't anticipated this, hadn't known what to expect I suppose. I let out a groan, part lust, part surprised delight.

"Count, Summer. If you miss I'll reduce the number of slaps to fifteen."

Bastard! He knows what he's about. "Sorry, Sir. One, Sir."

"At last. Now, pay attention." He delivers another ringing slap to my backside, and the balls lurch again.

My pussy is already starting to convulse.

"Two, Sir. I'm going to come again, Sir"

"No you're not. You've had your fun, now you can wait until I give you permission to climax."

"It's no good, Sir, if you slap me again I'm going to... Aaah!" I let out a startled scream as a hard slap lands on my already tender bottom. He means it now, playtime's over it seems, and this hurts. I don't forget his instructions though.

"Three. That really hurt, Sir"

"Good. Should take your greedy, slutty mind off climaxing again. You can thank me if you like." He drops another slap on my bottom, the other side now, this one equally hard.

I scream again, then return to my duty. "Four, Sir. Thank you."

"Feeling better? You're quite welcome, Miss Jones. Open your legs now please."

Groaning inwardly I do as I'm told, spreading my thighs as wide as I'm able and hoping he'll find it in him to be a little less severe when he slaps my pussy. The next slap lands directly on the swollen lips of my cunt. The balls deep inside me shift and gyrate, the inner weights spinning. He does relent, but only very slightly. The sensation is breathtaking, sends me lurching to the brink of the most powerful climax yet. I'm almost sobbing as I force out my next word. "Five, Sir. Please…"

"Would you like me to do that again, sweet little slut?"

"May I come, Sir? Please?"

He pauses, maybe he's considering my request. At last, he answers, "You may."

"Then yes, please do it again. Harder."

"My pleasure."

He slaps my pussy lips again, the blow hard, cruel, beautifully accurate. My body erupts in unbridled orgasmic pleasure as the balls are sent hurtling into a crazy, lurching rhythm, caressing my inner walls as my cunt contracts and spasms. I'm past all coherent thought, convulsing and shuddering as I lie helpless across Dan's legs, His hand is on the small of my back, holding me steady as he lightly caresses my quivering pussy, the gesture both intimate and caring.

I lose track of time, though it must only be a few moments later when the glorious sensations start to ebb. Dan's palm is circling my back, and I become aware he's talking to me. Murmuring something, soft, quiet. Achingly tender.

"That was number six. Are you ready for more, little sub?"

More? Is there more? Could there possibly be more? Apparently so. "Yes, Sir. Please."

"Close your legs, Summer. Brace yourself. I'm done being gentle."

The next slap lands quickly, on my right buttock. He's right, this is far from gentle. But I'm a credit to my tutor, remembering my instructions perfectly.

"Seven."

He continues to spank me, hard, unrelenting, and I continue to absorb the blows.

"Eight. Nine. Ten. Eleven. Please, Sir, may I have a rest? Is it alright to ask…?"

"It is, but you need to use your safe word, to make sure there's no mistake. Are you saying amber?"

"Amber. Yes, amber, Sir."

Dan's palm connects with my skin, sizzling from the spanking. He caresses my bottom lightly. "Lie on the sofa, face down. I'll get you some anti-inflammatory cream. Soon take the sting out of this."

He helps me to move, gingerly, sweetly tender, but even now the balls inside me are doing their thing. The inner weights cause them to swing and roll in a crazy rhythm as I sink into the buttery leather of the sofa. Dan's footsteps recede across the room. I watch through half-closed eyes as he picks up his sweatpants, discarded on the floor. He steps into them then disappears into the bedroom. He emerges a couple of minutes later with a tub of Savlon.

"I knew that brother of mine always keeps some of this stuff around. Shit, girl, your arse is a gorgeous shade of pink. All over."

"Thank you, Sir."

"My, aren't we polite? You've come a long way since we chatted in the bar at the Collar. I recall you were positively surly then."

He doesn't know the half of it. He sits beside me on the edge of the sofa. I say nothing, just wince as he slathers a generous handful of the soothing cream onto my bum. I lie still as he smoothes it into my skin, loving the cooling comfort as well as the tenderness in his caress.

"Is the spanking over, Sir?" I turn my head to look at him, over my shoulder.

He glances at me under his eyebrows, his expression wry. "I promised you twenty. Do you want the rest?"

"Could you not hit me as hard, Sir"

"Ah, so I've found your inner wimp have I. Well, I could ease up on you. Is that what you want?"

Actually, I'm not entirely sure it is, but I know my limitations. "I think so. If that's alright, Sir."

He nods sharply. We're agreed.

"Tell me when you want to go again then." He continues to stroke my bum, even though I'm sure the cream must be all absorbed by now. This is just for fun.

I stretch under his hand like a contented cat, and seriously consider purring. Dan's in no hurry, massaging my heated skin, soothing away the hurt.

Eventually I rediscover my enthusiasm for playing rough, start to crave the bite of pain he can offer. I turn to regard him over my shoulder again. "Please, I'd like the rest of my spanking now, if that's okay. Sir."

"Perfectly okay. Do you want to stay there or go back over my knee?"

"Could I stay here? Would that be alright?"

"'Would that be alright, *Sir*?' Don't spoil yourself now, girl. Not when your arse is so very vulnerable." The rebuke is delivered softly, but I know he means it.

"I apologize, Sir."

He gives a curt nod. "Bring your knees up underneath you, stick your bum up in the air for me please."

I do as he's asked me, the movement sending my little happy balls spinning again. I gasp, squeezing them with my inner muscles in a vain attempt to keep them still.

"Okay, no climaxing without permission. There are nine left, and this is how we'll do it. One on the left cheek, one on the right, then you spread your legs and take the third on your cunt. Then we repeat. Three times. Okay?"

"Yes, Sir."

"If you think you might come without permission, you can tell me that. I'll find a way to cool you down, though I can't promise that will be pleasant. You'd do better to control your response yourself if you can."

"I don't know if I'll be able to. Am I still counting?"

"It comes with practice. Try. And yes, you are still counting. Ready?"

"Yes, Sir." I drop my head, waiting for the first slap.

The sound is more severe than the sting though, as he delivers the first spank to my left buttock. He's certainly taken my pleas for clemency to heart.

"One, Sir."

He shifts his position slightly and lands the next slap to my right buttock.

"Two." I don't wait to be told what to do. I know the drill and open my legs as wide as I'm able, planting my knees as far apart as the width of the sofa allows.

"Turn around to face the back of the sofa. You can lean on that and spread your thighs wider."

I comply, repositioning myself as instructed. The Ben Wa balls make their presence felt again. I squeeze them hard.

"Your pelvic floor muscles will be getting a decent workout by now I daresay. How are you liking our little ball game."

"It's very nice, Sir. I enjoyed playing with yours earlier too."

"A shared pleasure, sweetheart. The best sort. Feel free to scream."

He lands a sharp slap onto my exposed pussy, and at this angle he is able to catch my clit too. I do scream, as he clearly knew I would, but it's more a cry of extreme emotional outpouring than of pain. This hurts, I have no illusions about that, but my level of arousal is off the scale. It's a pleasure-filled, exciting, addictive sort of pain, and I'm nowhere near done yet.

I close my legs unbidden, and groan as Dan drops the next two slaps on my buttocks, first the right, then the left. I spread my thighs to receive the next spank, my pussy throbbing now in anticipation. I'm wet, hot, desperate as I wait for Dan's palm to fall.

It does, but instead of the harsh slap I expected he draws a full-hand caress right across my swollen, sensitive cunt. His fingertips trail along the length of my clit, long, slow, seductive, and perfectly timed to cause maximum effect.

"Sir!" I scream, "I'm coming. Please, I have to…"

"Wait." The single word is imbued with such authority I sob in frantic dismay. I can't hold out, if he does that again I know I'll...

He does do it again. His palm presses firmly on my pussy as he strokes me, the pads of his fingers rubbing my clit before sinking into me. He nudges the nearest ball with his finger, and my muscles clamp down around his hand and the little eggs.

"No more. Please, you have to stop now. I can't..."

"Safe word or shut up. You know the rules, slut."

No way am I safe wording, and in any case he extracts his fingers and steps back from me. I'm reprieved. Briefly.

"Close your legs, girl. Last three now. You can come on the third."

"Thank you, Sir." I clamp my thighs together, still shaking from the powerful sensations coursing through me. I hardly let out a groan when Dan lands the final two spanks, as hard as any that have gone before but by now the pain is immaterial, subservient to the overwhelming bliss of expectancy I'm feeling.

I spread my legs as far apart as I'm able, leaning on the back of the sofa, my bottom raised as high as I can. I want this—I've earned it, waited for it. It's mine, all for me.

Dan does not disappoint. The last slap lands right across my clit and pussy, and sends shockwaves of pleasure tinged with agonizing pain shimmering through my body. I lurch forward, my orgasm surging up from deep in my cunt to pulsate sensuously, the sound of the slap still resonating as my body clenches and writhes in exquisite joy. Dan helps me, plunging his fingers inside me to stimulate and caress, drawing out the moment, extending the pleasure for me. He uses both hands, reaching one around to thrum my clit hard, the other plunging three fingers deep inside my pussy to roll and swirl the Ben Wa balls.

It's so intense, so fierce, I may have passed out momentarily. As reality solidifies once more, I'm aware that Dan has his arm around my waist, and is holding me upright when I would without doubt have collapsed in a heap. He draws the balls out of me, his movements slow. I gasp again at the sweet pleasure of being cared for so tenderly when I'm at my most exposed, my most vulnerable. Then he pulls me to my side and deposits me on the sofa, arranging himself so my head is in his lap. He combs his fingers through my hair, and I lie there, conscious only of the sound of my breathing as I nestle into the soft fabric of his sweatpants. No more words are spoken, none are needed. I drift off into a contented sleep.

Chapter Six

I stretch lazily, waking slowly. I can hear music, something classical by the sound of it, vaguely familiar. I roll onto my back, wincing slightly as my bottom connects with the soft leather. I'm pleasantly sore, aware of my body in a way I don't recall ever before. I'm still naked but a light quilt has been tossed over me, and I grasp it, snuggling back down. I feel wonderful. Better than wonderful. I feel alive, tingly and deliriously happy. Dan Riche is very good for my sense of well-being.

And talking of Dan, where is he? I crane my neck to peer round the room, or as much of it as I can see from here. He's nowhere in sight. I wriggle into a sitting position and peep over the back of the sofa. He's at the dining table, a mug of steaming coffee beside him. His smartphone is in his hand and he's tapping the screen. Catching up with his emails perhaps. Facebook? He glances up, and smiles at me. He's dazzling, quite stunning.

"You're beautiful." The words are out before I have an opportunity to censor them. A case of mouth slipping into gear before engaging brain. I clap my hand over my face, embarrassed.

Dan doesn't seem especially fazed by my comment. Maybe grateful women tell him he's beautiful every day. It wouldn't surprise me. He puts his phone down and gets to his feet, a quirky, lopsided grin on his face as he ambles back across the living room. He's still wearing just his sweatpants, his chest and feet bare. Prime male. My mouth waters.

"You're not so bad yourself, Miss Jones. Nice nap?"

"Mmm, how long was I asleep for?" I lift my tangled hair from my neck with one hand whilst hanging on to my quilt with the other, and stretch again. I have visions of not being able to sleep tonight, though I daresay Dan will find some way to wear me out if I ask him.

"Not long. Half an hour or so." He deposits his long body on the sofa by my feet, flicking back the corner of my quilt to make a space for himself. His hands encircling my ankles he lifts my feet into his lap and starts to massage my toes.

Christ! I thought his fingers on my clit were magical, but this is a close second. He grins at me, all sexy and rumpled and relaxed, tugging and squeezing my feet, stretching the muscles there and pressing his fingers into the soles. It should tickle, but it doesn't. It just feels simply divine. I'm wondering whether men like Dan Riche could perhaps be made available on prescription. It would save the health service a fortune in tranquilizers and sleeping pills.

I sigh and ease my body back against the sofa, stretching out and giving myself over to the hedonistic pleasure of a foot massage. Dan continues to work my feet, easing the kinks out of them just as he eases the kink into me, so to speak. Lovely.

At last, he breaks the contented silence. "Show me your arm."

"What?"

"Your arm. The patch test. Show me."

Ah, yes. The peppermint oil. I glance down at my arm, the skin unaffected by the liquid. Nothing to see at all. Dan nods in satisfaction.

"Excellent. Can you reach the dish? My hands are full." He gives my toes an extra squeeze, at the same time nodding in the direction of the small porcelain saucer still sitting on the low table. I stretch out my hand and can just get my fingertips to it. "Dip your fingers in and spread a little on your lips, please."

I do as he asked, my mouth flattening as the sharp, cool sensation seeps across my lips. It's a bit like holding a polo mint between my teeth. The super strength variety.

"How's that?" Dan lifts one eyebrow, watching my reaction with interest. I run my tongue over my lips, which are just starting to throb. Or should that be tingle? The sensation is one of heat and coolness at the same time, a curious combination. I explore with my tongue again, my eyes locked on Dan's dark gaze as the feeling intensifies, two extremes warring with each other on my lips.

"It's, oh, wow! That feels strange." No longer the cool polo mint, more the warm glow of aromatic spices. I rub my lips together, seeking friction, then lick them again. I can taste the mint on my tongue, but only faintly. The impact on my lips where I smeared the oil is building though, and I press my fingers to them, expecting to feel heat, or a chill. There's neither, but I rub anyway, only to find the sensation strengthens.

"Is it uncomfortable?" Dan is still watching me carefully as he continues to massage my feet. I glance up at him, wondering where this is leading, though I have a good idea.

"I want to lick my lips. All the time."

"Imagine how it will feel on your pussy. And your clit. You can't lick those lips. At least, not for yourself. Or maybe we could try it on your nipples…?"

I was right. I suppose now the only question remaining is 'when?'

I try for nonchalance, but privately I'm squirming at the prospect. My lips are throbbing now, the sensation not quite painful, but nowhere near comfortable either. The compulsion to rub, to lick, to stroke is becoming irresistible. "Well, I suppose you'd have to make yourself useful then…"

"Mmm, yes, I might. I'll tie you up I think. Your legs spread wide. Now that I know you're not allergic to the oil, and I've got the dilution about right, we can have some fun. Well, I can. I'll be interested to know what you think. Afterwards."

He lifts my feet from his lap and tucks them back under the duvet as he stands up. I'm expecting to be instructed to lie back and open my legs immediately, so I'm a little nonplussed to see him pick up the dish of oil and take it over to the kitchen worktop. He leaves it there, to return with a glass of water in one hand and my phone in the other.

"Here, rinse your lips. It won't make a lot of difference as that stuff's oil-based, but may help to soothe them a little. You have a text." He hands me the glass and waits while I take a few sips, using my tongue to splash water against my lips. He's right, the effect is minimal. The irritation, if that's the right term for it, is not increasing any more though, and I'm finding it quite bearable now I'm accustomed to it. Maybe my pussy will react in a similar manner.

Yeah, right. Dream on.

Dan takes the glass and passes me my phone. The blue light on the top is flashing, indicating a message is waiting for me. I tap in the unlock code and see it's from Ashley.

Hi Summer. Sorry to interrupt but I want to offer you a job? We need someone to organize things here, deal with admin, paperwork, company secretary, that sort of thing. Interested? If you are just let me know and we can discuss details when you're back. I'd like to get it tied up before Tom and I go away though. Please say yes. A xxx

I stare at the screen and read the message twice. Then once more, just in case I've somehow misunderstood. Then again, for good measure. Eventually I raise my eyes to Dan's. His head is cocked to one side, waiting.

"Wow."

My comment is not sufficiently illuminating. He frowns in puzzlement, though he doesn't say anything as he settles down by my feet and starts the massage again. I re-examine my phone, just in case the words have somehow rearranged themselves. They haven't. I'm still on the receiving end of a job offer.

"It's from Ashley. She's offering me a job." I look at the tiny screen again. Yes. A job. Me. *Shit!*

"A job?" Dan's tone is unruffled, he doesn't seem unduly surprised.

An insidious thought occurs to me. "Did you know about this? Have you put her up to it?" I don't mind him organizing my emotional and sexual well-being, but I don't want Dan sorting out my employment for me.

"Me? Not guilty, yer honor. But I did hear Ashley and Tom talking to Nathan and Eva so I knew it was a possibility. What *is* the job?"

"Sort of secretary by the look of it. Office manager. Organizing things."

"Sounds right up your street. Will you take it then?"

My head's reeling with possibilities. I like Ashley, and took to Tom straight away. Same with Eva. Nathan's scary, but so far he's been pleasant enough. The prospect of working with them all is appealing. I wonder where I'd be based. Ashley's text says she wants someone to organize things here so that suggests Black Combe, or Greystones. It's a lovely location, I could certainly get used to living in Yorkshire.

But what about Freya? My heart sinks in unexpected disappointment as I realize I can't just up sticks and move to Yorkshire. Only two days ago I promised her I was on my way home. And Dan lives in Cumbria too. Now that we're an item — well, I think we are. I look up at him, his gaze still on me as he manipulates my feet firmly.

"So? Will you be taking the job?"

"I can't. I can't just leave Freya. And what about…?" *Us? Is there an 'us'?*

"Freya's moved in with Nick, you'd be on your own anyway. She might decide to sell the apartment, or sublet it."

Dan's right, though I doubt that Freya would dispose of the property while I was still staying there. That wouldn't be fair, though, and I know that if she were not living in Kendal I wouldn't be either. I won't be homeless. I have my flat in Margaret's old house in

Ulverston. Freya had the place converted into four holiday flats, but she gave me the ground-floor one as a present for my twenty-first birthday. My bolthole she called it, because she knew how much I disliked returning to my mother's house. I've not used it much because I've mostly lived at Freya's, or in Bristol, but it's there if I need it.

I'm turning over the not especially welcome prospect of setting up home alone in Ulverston when Dan interrupts my thoughts again. "In any case, I think it was Freya's suggestion. She put the idea in Ashley's head, though from what I heard she didn't take a lot of persuading."

"What about you? I mean, would you mind...?" I'm not sure just what I'm asking here. Would he mind me staying in Yorkshire when he goes back to Cumbria? Would he mind me working for his brother's company? Would he mind me assuming he gives a damn?

"Sweetheart, I'm easy either way. I'm thinking of asking Freya to sublet her apartment to me, and if she agrees you're welcome to share it. But you won't be in the spare room any more. Or if you decide to stay in Yorkshire it's only a couple of hours away. I come down pretty often anyway to scrounge a decent meal from Grace. We'll work something out. It's up to you."

Share it? He's asking me to share an apartment with him. *Shit.* Now, there's an us. And here was me wondering if he'd even want to see me again after this weekend. I'm just gaping at him like an idiot, to such an extent that he casually leans across and places his fingers under my chin to close my mouth. My jaw snaps shut, and I continue to stare, incredulous.

"I never thought— I mean I didn't realize..."

"Me neither until just now. But it's a nice idea. Don't you think?"

"Which? I mean…"

"Both ideas are nice. It's your choice, love. But the offer of a decent job doesn't come along every day. And you can always come to Kendal at the weekends."

And he's right. I know he's right. We may need to compromise, both do a bit of work, but I can take this job and continue to see Dan. What's more, it seems Freya's been planning this all along, the cunning little cow. I'll have words with her, though not especially angry ones.

On impulse I pull my knees to my chest, dragging my feet from Dan's gentle hands, and squeeze myself. I'm squealing, giggling, hugging my happiness inside me. Is this what joy is like?

* * * *

Dan and I are snuggled in bed. The peppermint oil stayed on the worktop while we chatted about my job offer, and Dan's plans for moving to Kendal. He currently lives in a rented house in Keswick, but that's not convenient for his practice. He needs to be in South Cumbria and has been contemplating a move. If Freya doesn't want to sublet, he's thinking of taking another apartment in the same building, but not surprisingly he fancies the penthouse. I wouldn't lay money on her agreeing, she does love the place, but it's worth asking her.

I'm not sure where I'd live if I accept the job with Ashley. When I accept it—there's no remaining doubt in my mind. Dan tells me that between them Tom and Nathan own a dozen or more cottages around their properties so I'll have a choice. The text said nothing about accommodation being thrown in, but Dan seems pretty sure it'll be part of the deal. We'll see. There's a lot to iron out, but the main thing is, I want to give it a try. I texted Ashley back before we came to bed.

Thank you. What a lovely offer, and what a surprise. I'd love to work for you. When can I start? S xxx

She replied within minutes.

Soon as. Talk tomorrow. A xxx

So now I'm nestled happily in Dan's arms, my back to his chest, my bum tucked up tight against him. His cock is nudging my swallow tattoos, which feels appropriate for some reason. He pulls me closer, though I would not have thought that possible.

"I'm glad Ashley tracked you down."

"Me too, though I was intending to come home to Kendal anyway."

"Mmm, but would you have come back to the club?"

Good question. I think for a few moments. "No, I doubt it. You terrified me." Not strictly true, it was me that terrified me, not Dan. I turn in his arms, intending to set the misunderstanding straight. He loosens his arms around me to give me space to move, but that's all the leeway I get.

"I think we both know that's not how it was. I challenged you, pushed you, hurt you perhaps. But I didn't harm you. You didn't run from me, did you?" His voice is low and sexy, and although he's very much in Dom mode he's not seeking to intimidate me now.

His repertoire is most impressive. And effective. Despite his unthreatening manner I'm moved to apologize. "No, Sir. I'm sorry, I didn't mean that. Forgive me."

He drops a kiss on the top of my head. "You're forgiven, love."

"No spanking?"

"You'll save until tomorrow. Get some sleep now." His palm is on my bum, my swallows once more receiving some welcome attention as he caresses my skin.

I'm still pleasantly sore from our activities earlier in the evening.

"Thank you," I mutter, my nose pressed up against his chest.

"Do you know the collective noun for swallows?" His fingers are lazily tracing my tattoos as he drops the question, seemingly out of the blue.

"Mmm, yes, Sir, as it happens I do. I Googled it a while back."

"Yeah? Doesn't surprise me. What is it then?"

"A flight usually, or a gulp."

"A gulp of swallows? I like that." He pats my bum gently.

I wriggle under his hand, loving his touch. "There are more. You could have a kettle of swallows, or a swoop."

"A swoop? Makes sense."

"Yes. My personal favorite though, is a richness of swallows. That one's a bit obscure."

"A richness? That's gorgeous. A richness on your bum. And in my hands." To demonstrate his possession of my 'richness' he shapes his hand around my bottom, smoothing his palm across my tender buttocks.

"Yes, Sir, in your hands." I agree, as I drift off to sleep.

* * * *

I awaken before Dan. It's light, the morning sun streaming through the open curtains. We're on the top floor and short of a passing airplane, no one's likely to be able to see in so we saw no point in closing them. I lie still, enjoying the sound of Dan's gentle breathing behind me. He's curled around my back, his leg slung across my hips. One arm is draped over my shoulder, his fingers grazing my breast. I'm sure he's asleep, but even so, his touch seems deliberate, studied, intentional as ever.

I lift my eyelids to gaze around me. As I lie still, I start to notice other things about this room, details I didn't spot when I first came in here last night. There are solid beams spanning the ceiling, incongruous in such a modern structure. Several of them are sporting chunky-looking metal rings. No prizes for guessing what those are for. I know that the chest at the foot of the bed contains a dizzying array of sex toys, paddles and several canes, as well as rope and a number of leather straps. There's a chest of drawers at the other end of the bed, and I wouldn't be surprised to find that stuffed with consumables such as lube and condoms. And peppermint oil.

I squeeze my thighs together as I contemplate what the morning may well bring. He'll have to get a move on—we need to be leaving by around eleven I think, in order to be back at Black Combe for the board meeting which starts at one. This may be an informal gathering of friends, but I know that Nathan and Tom will expect everyone to be on time. Dan's a member of the board so is expected to be there. I'm not sure if I'll be allowed to attend, but I gather Freya's been invited. They'll be discussing the finance for the wind farm project which Tom has been working on. I know Freya has an interest in sustainable energy and is thinking of investing in the scheme, especially as by now she'll have explained to Nick that she has rather more in the bank than he may have imagined.

I roll onto my back, wondering how that conversation went. The movement reminds my bladder that it's been a while, and I know I'm going to have to make a move soon. A couple more minutes tick by whilst I drift happily between sleeping and waking, then the increasingly urgent signals from my bladder force me to extricate my snug and cozy self from the cocoon of duvet and Dan. I slither from the bed and make my way silently across to the en suite.

I've just reached the door when Dan's voice rumbles from somewhere under the covers, "Have one for me while you're there."

* * * *

"How long do we have." I'm sipping a creamy latte, which Dan has conjured up from the rather amazing coffee maker perched proudly on the kitchen worktop. I had a close look at it yesterday, but was unable to fathom out how to get so much as a gurgle from it. The machine looks so elaborate I wouldn't be surprised to learn it could launch a lunar expedition, but Dan has the measure of the gadgetry and has managed to produce a cappuccino for himself and a latte for me. We're lying on the bed, both naked, propped up on a pile of pillows.

"An hour or so. Just enough time for me to deal with you. I promised your richness a spanking, you'll recall."

I wriggle contentedly as my pussy moistens. "So you did. My poor swallows won't know what's hit them lately."

"Well, they have a choice this morning. My hand, a paddle, or maybe a tawse."

"What's a tawse?"

"A leather strap, split into two strands. Has quite a bite to it…"

I glance at him, and see a familiar wicked glint in his eye. Neither me nor my swallows may get any choice at all in this.

"I'd like to come to the meeting this afternoon, if that's alright."

He shrugs, seemingly not put out by the abrupt change of subject. "Of course. You'll be welcome."

"Thanks. And—I'd really prefer to be able to sit at the table without whimpering. I don't want everyone staring at me."

His smile is broad, his pleasure genuine. "Miss Jones, you are to be congratulated on your forward planning. It's clear that Ashley made an inspired choice when she offered you that job. The paddle then. But I'm borrowing a tawse from Nathan's box of tricks. We'll take it with us. You really do need to feel it wrapped around your delicate little arse before much longer. Now, drink up and lie across the bed."

I watch over my shoulder as Dan pulls his jeans on and zips them. He leaves the button unfastened as he rummages around in the chest before pulling out a heavy looking length of black leather. He tosses that onto the bed beside me. The tawse I suppose. It looks severe.

I clench my buttocks defensively as Dan crouches beside the chest again, and this time extracts a spanking paddle made of rubber, a deep scarlet in color. It looks a little like a table tennis bat, but it's flexible. He demonstrates that as he stands behind me, bending the instrument in his hands.

"Ten on each cheek, I think. Keep your legs closed for this."

There's to be no spanking my pussy this morning then, by the sound of it. And no application of peppermint oil either. This puzzles me.

"Sir, may I ask something?" Always worth a little caution at this stage, worth checking he's open to questions.

"Of course. Go ahead." Apparently he is.

"What about the testing you did yesterday, the peppermint oil? Are we going to use that?"

"I admire your enthusiasm, girl, but as it would be the first time I've done that with you I'm not sure how long the effects of the oil will last, and I wouldn't want to have to cut your session short. You would not bless me for it if that happened. Soon, though. Ready?" He flexes the paddle again, then slaps his thigh with it.

I stifle a pang of jealousy at the veiled reference to other submissives who must have preceded me. The submissives who he has used peppermint oil with. I suppose I knew, he's clearly experienced in this craft of his so must have gained that expertise somewhere. I just prefer not to have to think about it if I can help it.

"Yes, Sir." I roll onto my stomach, my hands stretched out across the bed, and relax to meet that welcome bite of pleasure mingled with pain as he paddles my bum.

Chapter Seven

The drive back to Black Combe passes quickly. Neither of us is saying much, but the silence is companionable and we are both contented enough I think. Well, I am, certainly. My bottom is smarting, and my pussy has a delightfully well-fucked burn to it as well. Dan is forceful and powerful as a lover, or Dom, and although I've been having a truly wonderful time my body is beginning to feel somewhat the worse for wear. I'm wondering if he might be persuaded to, I don't know, let me have a night off…

Even as that notion forms in my head I dismiss it. He won't, and I don't want him to. I shift in my seat, savoring my discomfort even as I wince. Dan slants a glance in my direction.

"The next time I fuck you, it'll be in your arse. And I intend to suck your clit until you plead with me to stop. Will that do, do you think?"

I don't waste so much as a moment wondering how he knows. He just does, always he does. "Thank you. That will be perfectly fine, Sir."

Dan just smiles, winks at me, and returns his undivided attention to the road ahead.

We arrive at Black Combe maybe fifteen minutes before the meeting is due to start. Nathan is already here, and Eva. So is Freya and I gather Nick just got here a few minutes before we did. He had to return to Cumbria yesterday to deal with some sort of hitch in one of his businesses, but he's returned in time for the meeting.

Dan and I stroll into the kitchen together, and by the eager expression on her face Freya is ready with her questions for me. She waits until Dan is distracted giving the car keys back to his brother, and no doubt explaining that he's also liberated a tawse from among Nathan's collection of pain play instruments, before she gives me a quick hug to say hello.

"Where have you been?"

I reply in sign, "Leeds."

She shrugs, opens her hands to signify a question. "Why?"

Still using sign I offer more explanation, "Nathan's apartment. You'd like it there." I'm ready to provide more detail, but from the look of delighted astonishment on Freya's face I suspect that may not be necessary. It would seem the fame of Nathan's fuck-pad has preceded us here. With a self-satisfied smile, I take an empty chair at the table, lowering myself carefully into it. I'm relieved that Nathan has seen fit to purchase nicely upholstered furniture for his home rather than the minimalist rustic-style hard wood stuff found so often in country kitchens. So much more submissive-friendly. Even so, I couldn't really describe myself as comfortable.

Dan takes a seat next to me, smirking. He passes me a folder from a pile in the middle of the table. I open it to find it's an information pack setting out the details of the proposed wind farm. I leaf through its contents, noting that Freya has also picked up a folder and is sitting down to study it intently.

Ashley and Tom are the last to arrive, and the gathering now complete the rest of the group join us at the table. Grace is not to be present this time, having decided to take Rosie and Isabella out for the afternoon instead. Her Clio is crunching across the gravel of the rear courtyard as Nathan calls the meeting to some sort of order.

He starts the proceedings by welcoming me, Freya and Nick. He goes on to assure us that the meeting will not be a formal affair and anyone who wishes to speak can do so. As I gaze at the others assembled round the table, I wonder if that remark carries more depth than face value might suggest. I know that Freya and Nick have a Dom/sub relationship, and based on his comments on the doorstep when I first arrived, I'm pretty sure Nathan shares those tendencies so it's likely Eva does too. Tom and Ashley? Probably. So the dynamics among the couples here are not solely concerned with business protocol but also with the power shift between Doms and their subs. Nathan's opening words are setting the tone, making it clear that, around this table at least, business is business. We are all individuals, all equal, and may speak freely. I appreciate the sentiment, though I don't expect I'll have much to say.

Freya will. I know she intends to participate in the discussion and I'm ready to interpret for her if needed though she hasn't asked me to. Or Nick might. By now he will be aware of her intentions and their smiling, affectionate presence indicates that he supports her decision to invest.

I volunteer to take notes of the meeting I hadn't intended to, but the task seems in keeping with my soon-to-be duties as company secretary. Might as well start as I mean to go on. It's an opportunity to show that I can make myself useful, and I feel a strong urge to demonstrate that fact, to prove to Ashley, and to Freya, that their faith is not misplaced. It also gives me a role in the meeting so I won't simply be observing in silence.

I dig a pen from my bag, and Nathan hands me a notepad. I'm all set by the time Tom gives us a brief outline of the project, and in particular, the funding gap that they are trying to bridge. It's all there in the information pack so I make sure I squirrel one away for future reference, but I jot down the main points too.

I gulp a little as Tom starts to rattle off the figures. Wind farms don't come cheap. The entire scheme will cost around eleven million pounds. Between them, Nathan, Tom, Eva and Ashley have just over five million pounds already identified, so they are nearly six million short. I'm wondering how much of that Freya will want to put in when Nick offers to chip in half a million. Nathan thanks him and makes a note. I do too.

Dan is next to volunteer a financial contribution. He offers another half a million, which is duly accepted. I note that on my pad reflecting that I've clearly been hanging around with Freya so long that I'm not even surprised that these people are bandying around six-figure sums as casually as if they were sharing the bill after a meal in a restaurant.

Nathan does a quick summing up. There is now six point two million pounds identified. He asks if anyone knows of any other potential investors before the consortium turns its attention to the banks. I'm not surprised when Freya taps the table, her signal that she'd like to speak. I turn to her, expecting to be required to interpret, but find she's looking straight at Eva.

Odd. Still, I can concentrate on note-taking. Through Eva, Freya offers to provide the balance of the money needed. She names the figures carefully and accurately, a sum not less than four point eight million, and not more than six point eight, depending on the final scope and nature of the scheme. I scribble this down, and consider the matter probably concluded.

There's a deathly hush in the room. The issue appears not to be settled. Nowhere near. Nick turns to Freya. "Six million quid! For fuck's sake, Freya, where would you get six million quid from?"

Hasn't he been listening to her? I know she must have told him by now, and in any case, what gives him the right to speak to her like that? Freya lifts her hands, clearly about to sign her reply. Her expression is one of apology, and my protective instincts surge to the fore. I won't sit here quietly while he puts her down. My words are blurted out before Freya has a chance to say anything.

"From down the back of her sofa probably." I glance around the room. "Why are you all looking so stunned? Six million quid is small change to Freya." I direct my final remark to her. "And it's about time you bought something useful. You can't just fritter away forty odd million on racehorses and trips to Australia."

Long, silent moments pass. I have a sudden, ridiculous vision of my words wriggling and squirming on the table, like a knot of slithering worms as we all peer at them distastefully.

Ashley is the first to speak. "How much? How much can't Freya fritter away?"

I look around the table, realization dawning too late, much too late. For reasons I can't even start to guess at, Freya has not told anyone about her money. Not even Nick. Incredibly, stupidly, for some bizarre and unfathomable reason, she hasn't told Nick about the millions salted away in her bank account. No wonder he's angry. I'm dismayed, mainly at my part in all this. Freya may have started this ball rolling, but I've just given it a huge shove. I just made everything a whole lot worse. Why didn't I just keep my head down and my mouth shut?

"Didn't they know? I assumed you'd have told them. Isn't that why we're here?" My words are whispered, directed at Freya who just shakes her head.

"I was going to tell Nick but I never got the chance." She turns to him, and continues to sign. "I'm sorry. I can explain."

Nick's response is to bundle her from the room pretty much bodily. Freya just has time to reiterate that her offer is a serious one, and that I can vouch for her ability to raise the funds. Clearly any explanation is to be delivered in private, and any retribution too. I know what's about to happen when he gets her alone. We all know, and I doubt any of us would dispute that punishment is deserved. But probably not here. Nathan won't stand for blood on his hall carpet, or for screams reverberating around his house. That stuff is confined to Leeds, though I don't doubt he'll make the facilities available should Nick wish.

The door closes behind them, and five pairs of curious eyes are now trained on me. My face is flushing, the heat radiating upwards. I can't believe the part I played in this debacle. Why didn't I just stay out of it? Freya didn't need my help, was well beyond anything I might have been able to offer in any case. I'm mortified.

I look first to Dan. His expression is not one of condemnation, just puzzlement. His lip is quirked in his familiar air of inquiry, his forehead creased as he tries to understand what just happened.

"I didn't mean to... I mean, I thought... I assumed you knew, all of you..." I'm stammering, not making a lot of sense at all. So much for impressing my future employers.

Dan reaches for my hand, removes the pen I've been gripping and wraps his palm around mine.

"She made quite an impression, our little Freya. Can you tell us what's going on?"

"I'm not... I mean..." I stare at our hands, linked on the table in front of me. I don't want to tell any more of Freya's secrets. I've never been disloyal, never intended to be this time. I feel awful, frankly terrible. I look up at him, my eyes pleading with him not to press me on this.

Maybe he picks up my signal, I'm not sure. The silence is broken by the slamming of a door upstairs, presumably Freya and Nick are now in their bedroom. I glance at Nathan, whose expression is decidedly pained. I hope for Nick's sake he doesn't do a lot more banging about in Nathan's house. He clearly doesn't like it.

Eva looks worried. "Nathan, do you think we should intervene? He might hurt her."

Nathan shakes his head, but his eyes are on Dan. "Nick's angry now, but he won't lay a finger on her until he's cooled down. Do you agree, Dan?"

Nick is Dan's friend rather than Nathan's. As Doms they all know the rules, but Dan knows Nick best and Nathan is looking to him to confirm that Freya is safe, at least for now. Dan has no hesitation.

"Absolutely. Nick will have plenty to say, but he won't actually punish her while he's angry. He'll make her wait."

Nathan nods slowly. I know Dan's probably right, but I'm still desperately worried. "Even so, do you think we should go up there? I mean, maybe I could help her to explain. Or Eva could…"

Dan shakes his head. "No, love. Leave it. They'll need to sort this out themselves."

"I know, but…" My words trail off. He's right. And anyway, I've done enough damage. We all fall silent for a few moments, listening to the raised voices — sorry, voice, from upstairs. My stomach churns nervously. Even though I can't make out the words I'd really hate to be on the receiving end of that tirade.

"So, what are these details you're going to fill us in on?" This from Ashley, who's been fairly quiet throughout the proceedings so far.

I gaze at her, my mind racing. I don't want to appear uncooperative, but this is really not my secret, despite what just happened. I'm not sure just how much information Freya wants me to provide. I need to talk to her first.

"I'm not sure, I mean, I can confirm that she's good for the money. She can afford to invest the amount she offered." I'm hoping that will be enough to satisfy everyone's curiosity for now, but without any great optimism. Ashley's eyes narrow. She clearly has a whole lot more questions.

"Did Nick say she won the lottery?"

He did briefly mention that, just before he ordered Freya out of the room so I suppose that much of the secret is out there too. I nod, and brace myself for the next salvo, but we're interrupted by a loud thumping from upstairs. Someone's knocking on the floor. We all stand, and Nathan's already halfway to the door when Nick's voice echoes down from upstairs.

"Summer! Get up here."

I shoot past Nathan, frozen in the doorway and bolt up the stairs. It takes me just moments to arrive at Freya and Nick's bedroom door. It's open, and I hurtle through to be met by the sight of Freya huddled on the floor, weeping in that silent way she has. Nick is crouching beside her, a phone in his hand.

I'm horrified. Dan was so sure he wouldn't lay a finger on her. Now look. I rush over, hurling abuse at Nick Hardisty, "You utter bastard. What have you done to her?"

He stands, turns to me. He doesn't react to my accusation. Instead he hands me the phone. "What do you make of that?"

I'm stopped in my tracks. Confused, baffled, I look at the phone. It's Freya's. There's a text on the screen. I'm dimly aware of others rushing into the room hard on my heels, of Eva and Ashley crouching next to Freya, of Nathan's angry tone as he rounds on Nick. Nick just lifts a hand, asking him to wait. He turns his attention back to me. "Summer, what do you know about this?"

I turn my attention to the screen, start to scroll through the texts. They are from a Malcolm Patterson, not a name I can place, but the upshot of the messages is that Freya's racehorse has had a fall at a race meeting and is about to be destroyed on the course.

As the significance of what I'm seeing dawns my heart turns over. Poor Freya. She adores that horse.

My voice dull, hushed, I confirm what he must already know. What Freya already knows.

My words spark a signing frenzy in Freya. Her hands are flying as she protests. "They can't, they can't. She's mine. My horse."

I drop to my knees next to her, my hands reaching for her stricken, tear-stained face as I try to comfort her, help her to deal with the inevitable. I'm dimly aware of Nick's voice, and Dan's as they discuss the catastrophe. Dan returns Malcom Patterson's call, then talks briefly to the course vet at Thirsk racecourse. The news is not good. Dan's expression is sympathetic but professional as he explains to Freya that her horse has a badly broken foreleg and that the best thing is probably to have her destroyed. Her racing career is definitely over.

Freya is just shaking her head desperately, refusing to accept the reality of what seems to be unfolding. Then, out of seemingly nowhere, another suggestion, this time from Tom. There's an equine veterinary center in north Leeds, and perhaps they could help. A quick discussion between Dan and the course vet confirms that this might be a solution.

Nick starts barking out instructions, making arrangements to transport the horse to Leeds and announces he'll drive Freya there. He asks Dan to come too, for his professional knowledge, and me as I seem to have some background understanding of what's happening. And, as he so delicately puts it, "If nothing else you can help Freya explain to me how the fuck she managed to buy a sodding racehorse right under my nose, and I never knew a bloody thing about it."

I somehow doubt I can come close to explaining that, but I agree to accompany them to Leeds anyway.

Chapter Eight

The drive to north Leeds is tense to say the least. Nick tosses the car keys to Dan as we dash across the graveled courtyard at the rear of Black Combe. He says he prefers Dan to drive as he knows where the equine veterinary center is. That may be part of it, but more significantly Nick clearly wants to talk to Freya. He gestures her into the rear seat of Nathan's lovely Audi, hastily commandeered as it's more comfortable for all four of us than Freya's Vanquish would be, and he follows her in. I'm left to sit in the front with Dan, an arrangement that suits me very well.

Nick's inquisition is pretty much unrelenting the entire way to Leeds. He demands to know how Freya came to be the proud owner of a racehorse without him having a clue. She does her best to explain, and where possible I chip in to support her side of the story.

I'm feeling absolutely dreadful for the part I may have played in this, though on calmer reflection I can see that Freya's deception was about to come out regardless of anything I may have said. I might have made things slightly more awkward, but that was unintentional. It never, not once, occurred to me that she would even contemplate going into that meeting not having told Nick what she had in mind.

Nick leaves the matter of the racehorse and moves on to the six-million-dollar question. Or should that be forty-six million? He wants to know why Freya seemed to feel there was a need for all the secrecy, and I have to admit I wouldn't mind getting my head around that too. I turn to watch Freya's signing, but don't find her explanation especially enlightening. It all seems to hinge around her having become so embroiled in her deception, that she lost sight of how she might ever end it. It became just too difficult. She ends up simply pleading with Nick to forgive her.

Neither Nick nor Dan can conceal their surprise when, in response to Nick's additional probing, Freya reveals the exact amount of money she won. Forty four million, seven hundred and thirty seven thousand, two hundred and ninety pounds. The car lurches as Freya signs it and Nick repeats the number, but Dan quickly recovers.

When we reach the equine veterinary center events move quickly. The X-rays show a compound fracture, serious but potentially repairable. The horse will never race again, but could live out a decent retirement. I suspect she'll be pampered something shocking if she comes through this.

Eventually, having done as much as we can at the center and leaving the horse in safe hands, Dan and I drop Nick and Freya at the entrance to Nathan's apartment in Leeds city center, the place we left only hours earlier. It will be more convenient for Freya to visit the equine center from here. I promise to bring her clothes over from Black Combe, and her car, as soon as I can manage it, tomorrow probably. I give her a quick hug, tell her not to worry too much about Queenie, not that she'll take any notice, then I hop back into the passenger seat next to Dan.

Dan smiles wryly at me as he maneuvers the Audi onto the M621, the urban motorway heading out of Leeds. "She's full of surprises, your friend. Got to hand it to her, I never would have guessed she was a multi-millionaire. And it's clear Nick didn't have a clue either." He shakes his head, and I'm sure he's as caught up as I am in trying to imagine the conversation probably going on between Nick and Freya at this moment. He looks across at me as he slows for some lights. "You knew the whole time?"

I nod, miserable at my part in today's events and painfully aware that I've been drawn into the deception too, though I have no idea what I could have done to avert any of this. Apart from keeping my mouth shut in the board meeting, of course. Dan doesn't seem aggrieved though, just surprised. And increasingly he seems to find the whole thing amusing.

Maybe I will too, in years to come. Perhaps Nick could, eventually. Freya even? But first, they have to settle their differences, and that prospect just scares me, particularly as I now have a pretty good idea what's likely to be involved. This is serious, much more serious than the punishment spanking Nick administered the night he and Freya met. I know she managed to come though that fine, and surely she and Nick are much closer now than they were then. He loves her, or seems to. He won't harm her. Will he?

"What'll happen now? Between Nick and Freya I mean." I shoot a glance at Dan, seeking reassurance.

He makes no pretense of not getting my drift. "He'll punish her. It *will* be physical. And severe, I should think."

"Will he hit her?"

"As in?"

"Will he beat her up?"

"No. Definitely not." Some comfort there, then.

Dan signals to pull out into the middle lane. He pauses for a moment to devote his attention to cruising past an HGV, then returns to his theme. "I don't know what Nick'll decide on, but it will be painful. Freya will learn a hard lesson, have no doubt about that. But he'll do her no lasting harm. And he won't do anything at all without her agreement."

Not that much comfort after all. And there's an aspect of all this so-called consent that bothers me.

"But she'll have no choice. Not if she wants to keep him."

Dan looks puzzled. "Why would you say that? Of course she'll have a choice."

"If she doesn't accept whatever punishment he decides on, he'll leave her. Won't he? Obedience is a condition of the deal, isn't it? She loves him. She'll do anything to keep him."

Dan slants another quick look my way. "I'm reasonably certain the feeling's mutual. I doubt Nick will be into ultimatums like that. But if she doesn't, or can't accept her punishment, it *will* cause a major shift in their relationship and I don't know how they'll resolve it. I really don't think it's going to come to that, though. They'll get past this. In time."

I fall silent to contemplate what he's said. He's right, I recognize that. Although I got off to a shaky start with Nick he does seem to adore Freya and without doubt came through for her when she had the awful news about her horse. In the circumstances that was impressive. Maybe this whole train wreck will turn out okay after all.

I'm reflecting on that optimistic thought when Dan breaks into my reverie once more.

"Do you want to talk to Ashley about that job? Or are you leaving it till later? I ask because I know she and Tom are intending to go off on their cruise soon. They delayed their honeymoon for a few days because Tom wanted to be at the meeting today, but they'll be gone by tomorrow. And they won't be back for at least a month."

"Oh Christ. I forgot all about that. Yes, yes definitely. Will they still be at Nathan's?" I want this settled, and ideally I'd like to start work immediately though I'm beginning to wonder if I might have to delay until they return. The prospect of rattling around on my own in Freya's apartment for the next few weeks is not appealing in the least, far better to be busy finding my feet with Darke Associates.

"Phone her and check. If not we can call at the farm. Unless you want to discuss it privately of course? I could just drop you off and pick you up later."

"No, I mean… Well, it's not really a job interview is it? She offered me the job, right? We're just sorting out the details now so I should think it'll be alright. I'd like you to be there, as long as Ashley and Tom don't mind."

Dan just shrugs and cocks an eyebrow in the direction of my bag. "Phone then."

A couple of minutes later I've established that Ashley and Tom are at the farm, that they are happy for me to go round to discuss the terms of my new employment, and that Dan is welcome too. And the kettle will be on.

* * * *

"We haven't really settled on a job title, but I was wondering about something along the lines of Projects Manager?" Ashley stirs her tea as she regards me across the table.

Tom is due to join us shortly. He and Dan are checking on one of his rare breed pigs that's gone down with swine flu or something.

I return her steady gaze, feeling slightly daunted. "That sounds grand. I thought you wanted me to just do the paperwork, admin, that sort of thing."

"We do, but most of the time there won't be someone around telling you what to do. You'll be running a lot of things yourself and just keeping us in the loop as needed. You'll be a manager, not a clerk. Generally speaking you'll report to me on stuff to do with the wedding venues project, and to Tom on the wind farm. Both Tom and Nathan are involved in the music festival, but that's mainly sorted now. Just need to actually run the event so it'll be manic while that's going on. We'll be back by then, but Nathan will want you to field the last minute stuff I expect."

I gulp nervously. It's not that I don't think I'm up to the job—details and organizing come naturally to me. I'll enjoy this and the more challenging the better really. It's bigger than I imagined though so I'm having to adjust my thinking, and clearly this is not a desk-based job.

"I'll need to buy a car." I'd been planning to, at some stage, but obviously it's a priority now. I intend to take Freya's Vanquish over to Leeds tomorrow because she'll be needing it to get to and from the veterinary hospital so I won't be able to borrow that.

Not that I feel comfortable using that huge, expensive beast. I'm too worried about bending all that shiny maroon metal. No, a sedate little hatchback is more suited to me.

"Transport comes with the job. So does accommodation. You'll need a four-wheel drive for out here. Especially in the winter." Ashley smiles at Tom, returning from his mission of mercy with the poorly pig, her expression one of quiet adoration.

Her look is returned as he drops a kiss on her hair on his way to the sink to wash his hands. Dan follows him into the kitchen. He nods at me, his smile warm.

"Nathan's Discovery does nothing most of the time. We'll see about borrowing that until we get something else for you," Tom tosses the words over his shoulder, commandeering Nathan Darke's expensive vehicle as casually as he might ask to borrow a pen.

"Right. Good thinking. I'll text him now." Dan drags his phone from his jeans pocket and starts typing the message.

Shit. Nathan Darke's shiny Land Rover Discovery. Now that I really mustn't bend.

"Did you sort out salary yet? And where Summer's going to live?" Hands duly sanitized Tom pulls out a chair and joins us at the table.

"No. But I was thinking we could start on twenty-five grand a year, maybe review after six months. How does that sound?"

I gape at her. Twenty-five thousand pounds a year! That's way more than I was earning as a librarian. Even with the rent for a cottage deducted, I'll still be quids in.

Tom gives a brief nod. "Sounds good to me. Is that okay with you, Summer? Plus accommodation and the car, obviously. Is your old place empty yet?" Tom directs his last question at Ashley.

I'm reeling again. Twenty-five grand *plus* a cottage, and the four-wheel drive too. This is too good to be true. Ashley smiles, probably amused by my expression of dumb amazement.

"Yes. Since all the wedding guests left we've got plenty of space. Smithy's Forge is lovely. I lived there when I first came here. Just one bedroom though? Will that be big enough?"

I'm on the point of saying yes, of course. It's just me, I'll be living alone so one bedroom is fine.

"Er, no. Actually, I'll need space for my sisters too." I intended to give the expected response but that's not what my mouth came up with when I got my words out.

Three pairs of eyes are fixed on me. I can't say I blame them. I'm probably more surprised than anyone. I've no idea where that came from. I've never planned to provide a home for my sisters. Not consciously in any case. And up until now I've not been in a position to. But now, I can. Just possibly. So I will. I'm ready to negotiate, to try to provide for them the security that Margaret gave me. The bolthole. The safe place to hide. Yorkshire's not as handy as Ulverston was, but it's do-able.

"How many sisters?" This from Ashley.

"Two. Lucy's fourteen and Maisie's eleven." I hold her gaze, willing her to understand.

"Where do they live now?" Dan's question is delivered in his normal low tone.

I only have to glance at him though to see his expression is intent. He can pick up on my nervous signals even if Ashley doesn't. I can almost see his antennae waggling

"In Barrow. With my mother. I'd like them to be able to come and stay with me sometimes. For holidays. Visits. I don't mind paying rent for a bigger place, I realize you can't be expected to…"

Tom interrupts me, his smile warm and reassuring, "Oh, I think we can manage something. In fact, the loft above Nathan's garage might suit you. Three bedrooms there. And he'd probably be happier with you living in it than renting to different strangers every week. Rosie'll like having other children around as well, even though your sisters are a bit older than her."

"You've not mentioned your sisters before. Are you close?" Dan's gaze is penetrating, his dark brown eyes fixed on my face.

Tom and Ashley are silent as all three wait for me to explain this sudden and unexpected shift in the arrangements.

"Yes. Fairly close. I don't see as much of them as I'd like so it would be nice if they could visit me here. Will that be alright?" I'm looking from Ashley to Tom now, almost pleading. "I'll keep them out of everyone's way." I have a suspicion that won't be easy, especially with exuberant, cheerful Lucy. But right now I'll promise anything.

"Don't be daft. They'll be welcome." Ashley is emphatic, looking to Tom for confirmation. It seems I have at least one ally.

"Aye, as long as they don't leave my gates open or dump crisp packets everywhere." Tom too seems ready to be tolerant.

There's one more, thing though, one thing I do need to say. "Lucy, the older one, well, she has Down's syndrome." I hesitate, not sure what to say next. I long ago gave up apologizing or making excuses for my gorgeous, bubbly, delightful sister. People need to accept her for the lovely soul she is.

Dan raises one eyebrow, I suspect my defiant tone is not lost on him. "So, you come as a package deal. Let me know when you want them to come down and I'll drive them. If that's alright with your mother, obviously."

I could hug him. I'm almost giddy with relief. Not that my mother will have anything to say about it. She'll probably not even notice they've gone, let alone who picked them up. "That'll be lovely. Thank you."

"Right." Dan returns to practicalities. "About this flat of yours. Nathan won't mind the flat being used for staff accommodation. I suspect that place would stay empty if you don't take it. How often do you think Lucy and Maisie will be here?"

I smile at him gratefully. "Not very often. School holidays mainly, perhaps odd weekends." Perhaps anytime my mother decides to expand her business again by bringing another one of her daughters into it. They're both too young still, much too young. She waited until I was sixteen, surely she would again. But I want to be ready. And Lucy's so vulnerable.

I don't say any of this, I'll never share the real reasons I'm so reluctant to ever return to Barrow, and so keen to help my sisters escape from there.

Dan's phone pings, signaling the arrival of a text. He picks it up, glances at the screen. "It's from Nathan. He says you can take the Discovery whenever you want. Grace has the keys. I'll just tell him we have an occupier for the garage flat…" He types in a reply then places the phone back on the table in front of him.

"So, we've sorted out your salary, your transport and now your accommodation. What else do we need to cover?" Ashley leans back in her seat, stretching as though uncomfortable.

Tom reaches out his hand to massage the back of her neck. The easy, familiar gesture is delightful, and I'm momentarily envious. Dan's lovely of course, especially now, over Lucy and Maisie. And he's been very nice to me. But our relationship is new, fragile. Tenuous. He'll be going back to Cumbria soon and I'll be staying here. No one will be around to massage my neck, or my feet.

Tom replies, all business and efficiency, "She'll need a job description, and a contract. We'll need bank details, national insurance number, that sort of thing. You'll have to sort all that out with Nathan as we'll be away. Agree a start date with him. You can find out when the flat'll be ready too. The refurbishment is almost complete but the place needs decorating and furnishing. You can stay here until it's ready if you like, or maybe you could stay at Black Combe. Black Combe's probably better because Grace'll feed you."

"Will there be an office I can use? I'll need a desk. Or should I work from home?"

Tom smiles at me, it's obvious he's been thinking all this through. "Both probably. We'll make sure you have a laptop and Wi-Fi in your flat, but there's also a small office here you can use, or the one at Black Combe. Again, I'd suggest Black Combe because it's bigger and Grace's lunches are legendary. Nathan only tends to be there on Mondays or Fridays, so you'll be able to work around each other.

I'm not sure about the prospect of Nathan Darke working around me, but I agree that Grace Richardson's home cooking is a key consideration, so Black Combe it is probably.

Chapter Nine

The short drive back to Black Combe passes in silence. For myself, I'm contemplating my extreme and unbelievable good fortune. Not only do I have a wonderful job suddenly, and a lovely home to go with it, but I've also managed to find a solution to a problem that terrified me so much I wasn't prepared to even acknowledge it.

My sisters will be safe. We'll all be safe, here in Yorkshire. I've yet to address the issue of permanency rather than occasional visits, as that is clearly my ultimate goal. It has to be. I'm doing this in bite-sized chunks but I'll get there.

And I've also got Dan Riche, for now at least. And Dan has that tawse, and his peppermint oil. We're in for an interesting time.

"Nathan will want to explain about Lucy, to Rosie. He may have questions for you."

"Lucy wouldn't hurt a fly!" I'm immediately on the defensive, though there was nothing even faintly threatening in Dan's tone or words.

"I know that. Nathan will too. But Rosie may not understand, especially if she's never met anyone with Down's before. He'll want to prepare the ground, make sure Lucy's made welcome here. Nathan cares about the people close to him, it's a failing we both have. That includes you now, and will include Lucy and Maisie too. I'm just saying, you're not on your own."

We're pulling up at the rear of Black Combe, and I turn to him in amazement, not for the first time recently. How does he know exactly what it is I need him to say? I suppose since Freya and I became friends I've not been on my own exactly, but this is different. Now I have even more friends, a lover, and my independence too. I can stand on my own feet, and support the people I love. I have a safe place to live, I'll have money of my own rather than sharing Freya's, and the future's what I choose to make it.

On impulse I lean across and kiss Dan full on the mouth. If he's surprised by my sudden demonstration of affection he hides it well. He tangles his fingers in my hair, returning my kiss enthusiastically. I slide my tongue between his lips, tasting the inside of his mouth, teasing and dancing with his tongue. He lets me play, then in a sudden twist he draws my bottom lip into his mouth and sucks on it. I gasp as my pussy moistens. Dan raises his head a fraction to break the kiss.

"So, I'm guessing you'll sleep with me again tonight?"

"Here?"

"Yes, here."

"Won't your brother mind?"

"Not as long as you don't scream and frighten his girls. Should I gag you?"

"You might have to, especially if you intend to use that leather thing."

"The tawse? No, I'm saving that. I have something else in mind for you tonight."

"The peppermint oil?"

"My, aren't you eager? No. That's something to be savored when there's no chance of anyone disturbing us. You'll have to wait and see. Come on, let's go and talk to Nathan about your new flat, find out when you can move in."

* * * *

Two weeks, it seems. The electrical work is almost done, fire alarms, light fittings and such like, and the decorators are booked for next week.

"Since you'll be living there you can choose the furniture if you want. We usually buy stuff from Ikea. Grace normally deals with all that side of things, curtains, carpets, cushion covers. If you don't want to be bothered with it I'm sure she'd be happy to do it all, but we just thought…" Eva's voice trails away as she pours tea for the four of us in the comfortable living room at Black Combe.

It's a scene of relaxed domesticity. Nathan is lounging in an easy chair, Eva kneeling on the floor at his feet as she busies herself with teacups and the sugar bowl. Dan and I occupy the sofa opposite them.

Grace is upstairs supervising Rosie's bath. Baby Isabella is also upstairs, asleep in her cot. Nathan has the baby alarm at his elbow. He leans forward to take his cup from Eva, his eyes on me. "So, Summer, when do you want to start work?"

"Can I start in two days? I promised to take Freya's car over to Leeds. I know she'll be needing it so I was planning on doing that tomorrow. And yes, I would like to choose some of the furniture, if you're sure that's alright."

Eva nods thoughtfully. "That could work out well. What about, you drive the posh car over to Leeds and I follow you in my Mini? We can say hello to Freya, find out how the horse if doing, and, well, everything else. Then we can hit the furniture showrooms. Grace could come too if she wants. And Freya if she's up for it. It would be a girls' day out."

Eva doesn't actually say so, but I know we're all dying to know how things are between her and Nick, if they've managed to settle their differences yet, and at what cost to Freya's backside?

Eva continues her planning, "The master bedroom in the garage flat is huge. I know Grace had been thinking of a four-poster bed there. Tourists like that sort of thing, but as it's going to be your home, well, maybe you prefer something else?"

I glance up, open my mouth to suggest maybe something a little less showy, but Dan is there ahead of me, "A four-poster sounds excellent. We'll stick with that."

I turn to him, puzzled, in time to catch the wicked glint in his eye.

Nathan takes a sip of his tea before offering any comment. "Yes, definitely a better choice. Four-posters are good for tying subs to. I'm thinking we should get one, sweetheart." He winks at Eva.

"I like the bed we've got. It's very comfortable." She's making an admirable effort at maintaining her composure. And her dignity.

"I don't think comfort's what we're going for exactly. That settles it. Get two four-posters." Nathan places his cup on the low table in front of him, then settles back. He exchanges a look with his brother, who immediately picks up the theme.

"Definitely. And we'll need silk rope too. Less chafing. Would you prefer that in red or black, Summer?"

It was Eva's misfortune to choose just that moment to take a sip of her own tea, which she manages to spray pretty much everywhere. There follows a fit of furious coughing, and Nathan leans forward to pat her between the shoulder blades, his expression solicitous. He casts a baleful look Dan's way.

"Now look what you've done with your dirty talk. You've brought on my sub's asthma." He reaches into his jeans pocket and retrieves a blue inhaler which he shakes before offering it to Eva.

She takes a couple of puffs and matters seem to settle down quickly. Wonder drug or what? Despite his casual air, I'd say Nathan looks concerned, but as Eva's breathing returns to normal he switches his attention back to Dan and I.

"So, the day after tomorrow then? To start work?"

I gape at him, my head still reeling from the previous exchange, my pussy moistening treacherously as I reflect on the prospect of being tied to Dan's bed with silk rope. Or more accurately it seems, my own bed. Inspired by Eva's valiant if ill-fated efforts I manage to rally. "Red please. For the rope. And yes, the day after tomorrow. If that's okay with you. And I'd love to check out furniture tomorrow."

"Right. When Grace comes down we'll find out if she's able to go too. She'll be handy to have with you, she has all the dimensions and so on." Nathan picks up his cup again, at the same time gesturing to Eva to take another puff of her inhaler, for good measure.

"I'll make sure I'm here, at least for your first morning in the job, to show you where everything is and help you get settled. Will you be using the office here?"

"I was hoping to, but I don't want to be in your way."

"Plenty of space." He flaps a hand at me airily. "So, we know you're good on the admin and organizing side. Have you had any accountancy training?"

"No, I'm sorry, I haven't. Will that be a problem?" *Please, no. Not when everything is working out so well.*

"I think it'd be helpful if you did. Would you be up for that?" His dark gaze is serious now, his business demeanor completely overshadowing the playful, teasing Dom who emerged a few moments ago.

I respond in similar vein, "Yes. Certainly. I've never considered accountancy before, but I can see it would be an ideal fit with my existing skills. A good career development move."

"Right. I'm glad you see it that way. Perhaps you could research what's available locally and let us know how you want to incorporate some additional training then. And flag up any other training needs too. Job related, naturally." The Dom had not entirely disappeared it would seem. "Now, I'm assuming you'll be staying here with us until the flat's ready? In Dan's room?"

I open my mouth to reply, though with no concrete notion of what I'm about to say. Dan's interruption is not unwelcome, at least it gives me more time to think.

"Oh, *my* room is it now?" Dan's grinning widely, the mercurial exchange not lost on him it would seem. "I seem to remember you telling me I make the place look untidy, and not to make myself too much at home."

"You do, and you tread muck in. You *and* Tom. But you never take any notice of what I say, and I've got used to it now. The place is overrun with women and kids most of the time and I need a bit of male company, even if it's only you. I suppose you'll never be away from the place now that Summer's going to be living here?"

My head snaps up. I'm glad Nathan asked, I think. I never would have dared. At the same time I'm dreading Dan's response. We haven't discussed anything beyond the next day or so, although I suppose he did casually suggest I could move into Freya's apartment with him, if he manages to talk her into letting him have it. Grounds for optimism, surely.

He turns to me, appears to be considering carefully, though his lecherous grin is unmistakable. "Well, a four-poster bed, red silk rope and a beautiful submissive. It'd be rude not to."

Not exactly the reply I was hoping for, but shows promise.

"And yes, Summer will be in my room. Is that alright with you?"

Nathan just nods briefly. "Your choice. Both of you. You know my rules about keeping it away from the children, though. And Grace too if possible, although she does tend to have a knack of always knowing what's going on. Talking of children, I gather we'll be having young visitors across in the flat."

Another shift in the conversation—I do find these men difficult to keep up with. Eva's clearly had more practice. I get my brain back in gear fast.

"Yes. My sisters." I remember Dan's comments about Lucy. I suppose now's as good a time as any... "I should say, or rather, I ought to tell you, one of my sisters, Lucy—she's fourteen—has Down's syndrome."

I just blurt it out and leave it hanging. By now I really should have learnt to handle this better. Both Eva and Nathan regard me quietly for a few moments. Nathan responds first, "I see. And does Lucy have any particular health issues then? Anything else we should know about? Look out for?" His tone is serious now, no teasing here.

I appreciate it, this is a sensitive area for me, as it probably is for all families like ours.

"No, not especially. A lot of Down's children have heart defects, but so far Lucy's been fine. She does tend to be rather…affectionate though. She's big on hugging, is Lucy."

Nathan grins. "I'm sure we've all been guilty of that, at times. She sounds lovely. Make sure you bring them both over to the house to say hello to us all, first time they visit here. Rosie will love to have other girls nearby."

"What girls? Who's going to be nearby?" Rosie comes bounding into the room, Barney and Grace in her wake. She's wrapped in a huge towel, her hair still dripping from her bath. She hands a comb to Nathan and clambers onto his knee.

Wordlessly he starts teasing the tangles from her hair. I get the impression this is their regular ritual after her bath.

Nathan deals with her questions. "Summer has two younger sisters. When she moves into the flat over the garage, they'll be coming to visit her sometimes. How old did you say they were, Summer?"

"Eleven and fourteen."

"I'm ten. Well, almost ten. Do they like Barbies?" Straight to the important stuff, young Rosie.

"I expect they will. Doesn't everyone?" Eva hands Grace a cup of tea as she joins in the conversation, her coughing fit now completely subdued once more. "We'll invite them to tea. Would you like that, Rosie?"

"Yes. But there'll have to be cake. And chocolate crispies."

"I'll make the cake, you're in charge of crispies. Right. That's settled then. You're all coming to tea." This from Grace as she helps herself to sugar, her smile warm and welcoming.

I pick up my cup and sit back, the careless family chatter and affectionate banter swirling around me. I think I'll like living here.

* * * *

"Time for bed, Summer." Dan bends to murmur the words in my ear as we share the washing up.

It only really amounts to rinsing plates and stacking them in the dishwasher, but it's a pleasant, homely, companionable task. I enjoy it. Nathan has a rule that Grace is off duty after we eat our evening meal. She cooks, but doesn't clear away or do any other housework. She still officiates over Rosie's bath occasionally, though Eva usually gets that honor now. Grace normally gets to spend her evenings with her feet up watching soaps and TV dramas while Nathan, Eva or Dan rattle the pots around.

The lines between employee and family member are blurred here to the point of being almost non-existent. Dan tells me he can't recall a time Grace ever took a holiday, apart from when she's gone with Rosie and Nathan in the past, and those trips now include Eva and Isabella. It's interesting to note that Grace still calls her employer 'Mr Darke', but Rosie calls the housekeeper 'Nana'. No one seems to mind, it all works. And now it includes me. And perhaps, just possibly, I can manage to extend all this to encompass Lucy and Maisie too. The invitation to tea is a good start.

First things first, though. Bed, with Dan. Now.

"Yes, I am tired."

"Too bad. You won't be getting a lot of sleep. I have to go back to Cumbria tomorrow so I intend to make the best of you while I'm still here."

I turn to face him. "Tomorrow? Oh. When will you be back?"

"I normally come down here very six or eight weeks or so..." He smiles, clearly impressed by my crestfallen expression. "Will you miss me, little sub?"

"Well, I expect I'll be busy..." I certainly hope so. *Eight weeks. Shit!*

"Not the right answer. You're supposed to beg me to stay, or to come back soon. You should be offering me the use of your body in any way I like. You're supposed to drop to your knees, naked, plead with me to fuck you." Dan injects a note of what I think is probably mock sternness into his tone. It's hard to be sure.

"Would that help? And if I did all that, how would I manage to fit in the accountancy course?"

He slaps my bum, in play perhaps but hard enough to hurt. "Enough with the pragmatics. I want you naked and kneeling. On my bed. You have two minutes."

"But what about..."

"One minute, fifty-five seconds. I *do* still have that tawse, Summer."

"Of course, Sir." I head for the door, my hand drifting to rub my sore bottom. I suspect it will get worse before it gets better.

Chapter Ten

It's a scramble, but I manage to get my clothes off and position myself in the center of Dan's large bed just as his tread sounds on the landing beyond the door. My eyes are downcast, but I swivel my gaze just enough to see the door handle turn. Dan enters. I continue to keep my gaze lowered so he is only visible to me from the waist down. His jeans are stretched tight, the beginning of an erection already apparent. It delights me that just the thought, or perhaps sight of me is sufficient to cause this reaction.

I'm kneeling, naked as instructed, my hands resting palms up on my thighs. I'm intrigued to note that just assuming this position puts my head in the place it needs to be, ready, willing, submissive. And with a delightful fluttering of butterflies low in my stomach. I'm placing myself in Dan's hands, certain I'll be safe there. I'm nervous, but not afraid. Anxious, anticipating, eager. Excited too. Every encounter with my Dom is better than the one before it seems to me, and growing familiarity has brought with it a contentment and confidence I never previously dreamed of.

I draw in a deep breath as Dan circles the bed, viewing me from all angles. I let it out slowly, draw in another.

"You are beautiful. Quite lovely. Your submissive pose is perfect. Well done."

"Thank you, Sir." I maintain my stillness as he approaches behind me.

His breath is a light caress on my shoulder as he draws close. I start, but only slightly, as he trails his fingers across my tattoos.

"A richness of swallows. I love your bottom, Summer. So pale and pink just now. But later…"

Later. The butterflies' fluttering increases to a frantic, agitated flapping as my lively imagination takes control of my body. I'm already visualizing his handprints on my bum, anticipating the sharp sting as he spanks me.

"Please, Sir, I…"

"In a hurry, Miss Jones? Is there somewhere you need to be? Am I keeping you up, perhaps?"

"No, Sir. I'm sorry." We'll be going at his pace. We always do. I fix my eyes on my thighs determined not to earn myself another reprimand, however gentle.

Dan's palm is soft against my bottom. He caresses my beautiful swallows slowly.

"A richness? Sounds about right. I wonder if we could improve on it, though. How about a gorgeousness of swallows? Or a perfection?" His voice is low and incredibly sexy.

I might dissolve into a puddle right here and now. Certainly my pussy is moistening, the dampness already noticeable under my bum. He has only to slip his hand a little farther round, just slide his fingers under me, between my sensitive folds, and he'll know it too. Except he probably already does. He always knows.

I shiver, every nerve ending attuned to his touch, his seductive voice. I don't reply, unsure whether I should. It seems not to matter

"What would you like me to do to you, Summer? Do you want pain tonight? Or pleasure?"

Now he does require some input from me. "Can't I have both, Sir?"

"That's greedy. Choose."

I don't hesitate. "Then I choose pain, Sir."

He caresses my bottom again, moving his attention to the other cheek now and abandoning my swallows. "You surprise me. Why choose pain?"

I give him an honest answer, and one that surprises me even as I say the words, "Because you're going away, Sir, back to Cumbria. This may have to last me a while. I want tonight to be — memorable."

"It will be. And I won't be gone long."

"Six weeks seems like a long time to me. Maybe even eight weeks." I don't want to sound whiny, or clingy. But I *will* miss him. Terribly.

"I'll be back in ten days, maybe less if I can find a locum."

I turn my head to meet his eyes, puzzled. "But downstairs, you said you wouldn't be back for six weeks. Maybe even as long as eight."

"Did I give you permission to look up, Miss Jones?" The timbre of his voice alters, only very slightly, but the edge is there, the clipped coolness of a Dom who intends to be obeyed.

It works, and I fix my gaze firmly back on my thighs. "I'm sorry, Sir. It won't happen again."

"Concentrate. I don't want to have to discipline you this evening, but I will if it's needed." Still that hard, implacable tone.

My bottom clenches under his hand as he continues. "What I actually said was that I wouldn't usually be back for six weeks, maybe eight. But that was then, before I had an incentive to come to Yorkshire more frequently."

Me? Does he mean me?

He leans in to murmur in my ear, "You are one powerful temptation, Miss Jones. I think my brother's going to be sick of the sight of me cluttering up his house. Or maybe I'll just need to spend all my time at the flat over the garage."

Yes! I know I'm smiling though he won't see unless he chooses to look closely as I keep my eyes obediently lowered. I manage to keep my voice even as I reply, "You'll be very welcome, Sir. Should I stock up on condoms?"

There's a pause. I wonder if I've overstepped the mark, been too pushy. Then he leans in again, his breath brushing the back of my neck. "You do that, Miss Jones."

"So, are you still looking for pain, little sub?"

"I'm not so sure now, Sir. Could you decide please?"

"A little of both, perhaps. Hold out your hand."

I do as I'm told, without hesitation. He drops a small handful of metal objects into my outstretched palm.

"You know what these are?"

I nod. *Nipple clamps. Ouch.*

"Okay?"

Another small nod from me. I know this will be alright, Dan has never let me down. I want to try everything he has to show me.

"Good girl. I'm going to tie your hands behind you now."

He holds out his hand and I relinquish the nipple clamps to him. He tosses them onto the bed. As the objects scatter across the duvet I notice there seem to be three items. I look up at Dan, puzzled.

"A clit clamp too. A special treat." He winks at me.

I relax. Slightly. And shiver. A lot.

"Place your hands behind you. I'd like you to grasp each elbow with the opposite hand but I'll put you into position this first time. In the future you need to remember it. This is what I want you to do when I ask you to present your breasts to me."

"Thank you, Sir." I reach back, laying my hands, palms down on the duvet behind me.

I can hear Dan moving around, though I'm careful not to turn to watch. There's the sound of a drawer opening, then closing, and he's back, standing behind me. He takes my hands and gently bends my arms at the elbows, positioning me to his liking. My palms are cupping my elbows, and he quickly ties my forearms together to hold me in that position. He's using something quite soft, scarves perhaps.

"Is that comfortable? Not too tight?"

"It's fine, Sir, thank you."

He plunges his fingers into my hair, lifting and turning my head. Leaning around, his eyes are close to mine, his gaze hot and appreciative. He places his lips over mine, his kiss deep and sensual as mine part under his. I suck his tongue willingly into my mouth, loving the questing sensation as he tastes, tests, explores. His tongue strokes mine, trailing behind my teeth and along the most sensitive part of my lips. I tilt my head back in welcome, my eyelids dropping as I sink into the intimacy of the moment.

I have no power to break the kiss, even if I wanted to. Eventually Dan raises his head to murmur in my ear, "So sexy, so submissive. I adore you, Summer."

Adore? Is that the same as love? It'll certainly do for now.

"Ready to continue?"

"Yes, Sir." My voice is thin, breathy, the butterflies now in full flight low down in my belly.

Dan smiles and straightens, then walks around to the other side of the bed. Now he's facing me, his expression deep, intent. He sits on the edge of the bed, reaches for the nipple clamps. They look a little like hair grips, but with a sliding bead holding the two arms together. Dan demonstrates them to me.

I'm going to slip the clamp over your nipples, then slide the bead up to close it. When it's as tight as you can bear, you tell me and we stop there. They're meant to hurt, but not too much. At least, not this first time." He glances at my already swollen nipples. "I see you're getting in the spirit of this, Miss Jones. I need to perk you up a little more still though. May I?"

"Of course, Sir. Please." *So polite.*

He smiles his thanks, then takes my left nipple between his fingers. He squeezes and tugs slightly. The position of my arms has pulled my shoulders back and thrust my breasts out to him. His eyes are on my swelling, now throbbing bud, hardening in his hands as he rolls and squeezes it. His grip is sharp, the intention to hurt. I hiss as the pain bites, and he glances sharply up to meet my gaze.

"We've hardly started, Miss Jones. If it's easier for you not to watch I won't insist. Close your eyes, and concentrate on breathing evenly. Don't move, and don't struggle."

I nod, not trusting myself to speak, and close my eyes. Dan returns to his task, increasing the pressure on my nipple until I'm grinding my teeth with the effort of not crying out. My instinct is to shrink away from him, but I know he won't take kindly to that. I've learnt enough by now to know that only my safe word will stop this, and I don't want to use that. Yet.

"Tell me when it's amber. When you're almost at the point of safe wording, I want to know."

"Now, Sir, it's amber now," I blurt out the words, conscious that my eyes are watering and my mouth trembling. This is more difficult than I imagined. The pressure is not relieved, but neither does it increase any more. My swollen, tortured nipple is still compressed between Dan's fingers but he's no longer twisting and pulling.

"Breathe through it. It won't hurt any more than this, and this is only amber, not red. You can do it. Open your eyes, love, and tell me you can do it."

His tone is soft by still commanding. I have to obey. I prise my eyelids open, my tears now unchecked as they flow down my cheeks. Dan ignores my apparent distress. Tears will not stop this either. I look at him, his image distorted in my watery gaze, and simply nod. I watch as with his free hand he reaches for one of the nipple clamps beside him on the bed. He opens the two arms, one handed still as he has not released my nipple, and slides the clamp over the distended peak. The ends of the clamp are coated in a softer material, silicon or rubber to protect my delicate nipples. *So considerate.* He slips the bead up the length of the clamp, forcing the two arms together around my tip. Only then does he let go with his fingers.

"Tighter?" He tips my chin up so he can see into my eyes. I don't know what to say, but it seems he's taking his signals from my expression anyway rather than my words. "Maybe a little?" He lifts one eyebrow, and interprets my silence, correctly, as consent.

His fingers deft and sure he eases the bead a fraction higher, increasing the bite by just a hair's breadth, but it's enough to push me to the edge of my endurance.

"Amber…" I whisper.

"Yes, amber. Now for the other one. Do you want to close your eyes again?"

I do. This time seems quicker, perhaps because I know what to expect. Dan's handling of me is cool and efficient. There's nothing cruel in his treatment, despite the pain he creates. His attention is focused wholly on me, on my responses. I know he's aware of how I'm feeling even before I tell him. But I also know I have to use my safe word, he won't stop otherwise. I bear the pressure, the pinching and merciless pulling on my tortured bud for as long as I can, concentrating on breathing as he told me before. When I can take no more, I mutter the one word that will stop it.

"Amber."

This time, when I open my eyes, less tearful now, Dan drops a swift kiss on my lips. He doesn't relinquish his tight grip on my nipple but he has stopped ramping up the pressure in response to my safe word. I watch in curious detachment as he slips the clamp on and slides the bead up to tighten it. His dark chocolate gaze never leaves mine until my lips part to tell him amber again. He stops, waits for the word, then sits back to look at my clamped breasts.

"Very pretty. Exquisite even. Do you agree, Summer?"

I look down, and despite my discomfort, which is actually diminishing by the second as my body adjusts, I have to agree with him. The nipple clamps are delicate and attractive, designed to decorate as well as create that vivid sensation I am starting to love. My nipples are tingling, they feel super-sensitive. As if reading my mind, Dan leans forward to blow on my right breast. His breath is a soft caress, trailing seductively over my tender peaks.

I gasp as he flicks with his tongue, first one side, then the other. It feels so much more intense now, almost unbearable. With his eyes raised to hold my gaze, he takes my right nipple, the first one he clamped, between his lips. He holds it there, trailing the tip of his tongue across the swollen, hard bud in a gossamer light caress.

"Oh, Sir..." I hadn't intended to cry out, but couldn't help it. Immediately conscious that we're not alone in the house I bite my lip to prevent any further such lapse. I don't suppose Dan will have any hesitation in gagging me, if need be.

He shifts his attention to the other side, taking my left nipple into his mouth. This time he sucks, his touch light and delicate, but with devastating effect. His fingers are on my other nipple, brushing the tip with the softest of touches, just feathering across the sensitized skin.

I lean back, not to escape, but because I'm no longer able to support myself. Dan allows it, shifting with me as I lie on the bed, my arms still tied securely behind me.

I'm moaning, writhing on the duvet, Dan's mouth and fingers flicking and caressing my breasts. He palms the lower curve of my right breast to hold me still, lifting the clamped nipple to his mouth. He increases the suction, now grazing with his teeth. I'm silently praying that he won't bite me, and at the same time pleading for him to. Mercifully, he doesn't, at least not yet. He releases my peak and rolls to lie alongside me, propped on his elbow as he looks down at my face. He feathers the backs of his knuckles across each of my quivering buds, smiling as I arch under his hand.

"Just a few more minutes, this first time. Shall we try the clit clip now?"

"Does that hurt as much? When you put it on?" *Not that this will stop me. Just asking.*

"No, clit clips are for fun. Jewelry almost. May I?" He picks up the one remaining object, this one shinier than the nipple clamps. It looks to be made of gold, or some metal similar in appearance, and has glittering beads dangling from the end of each arm.

He smiles at me. "You'll love this. Spread your legs wide."

I do it instantly, bending my legs at the knees and planting my feet as far apart as I can. Dan taps my ankle, signaling me to shift my foot a bit higher toward my bum. I do that, mirroring the action with my other leg. Sitting alongside my hip now Dan turns to face slightly away from me. He leans to get a better view of my pussy, which I know must be gleaming decadently and thoroughly wet.

"Someone's eager. I brought some lube, but we won't be needing it." To illustrate his point he draws his fingers the length of my pussy, from my arse to my swollen clit.

My response is a strangled sob. I so don't want to be gagged, but much more of this…

"Did that feel good?" He turns to regard my face.

I nod franticly.

"And this?" He does it again, but this time slowing the motion and dipping his finger tip into my entrance. He glances back at me for confirmation.

"Dan, please, I…"

"Sir. It's Sir when we're in a scene. Pleased try to remember that, however aroused you are. Now, answer my question."

"I apologize, Sir. Yes, it feels fabulous."

"I agree. And you look fabulous too. You'll be even more beautiful wearing this." He places the clit clip on my stomach, returning his attention to my throbbing pussy.

"Would you like to watch this?" He turns to face me again.

I frown, uncertain what he means.

"Don't move a muscle. He stands and goes over to the en suite, returning moments later with a round shaving mirror. The magnifying type. He positions that on the bed, angling it to provide me with the best view possible.

"Okay?" He raises one enquiring eyebrow.

I lift my head to be able to look in the mirror, and nod my agreement. I do indeed have a splendid view, my pussy in all its cherry-pink glory, aroused and throbbing, spread out for my Dom.

Turning slightly away from me again he parts my inner lips with one hand, peeling back the hood which shields my clit to display it proudly. I watch, fascinated, unsure whether his touch is more arousing, or the sight of his fingers stroking and opening me. It's immaterial, the combined effect is devastating.

"Sir, I'm going to come. May I…" He hasn't told me not to, but I'm conscious of the need to seek permission.

"No. You'll wait until the clip is in place."

"I don't think I can. Please, Sir, if you touch me like that I can't help …"

"You know I'll touch you however I please. And you will remain still, and only orgasm if I give you permission. You know I'll punish you if you come before I tell you to, don't you?"

I chew on my lip, closing my eyes against the erotic sight of Dan's hands caressing my exposed clit. Desperate, I cast around the far reaches of my brain for a list to write, or maybe I could try to recite the alphabet backwards.

"Don't you dare, little sub. I want your full attention. Now."

How does he know this stuff?

His tone is hard, cool, all Dom. I open my eyes, but my gaze is on him now rather than the mirror. All my senses are attuned to what he's doing to me and on my desperate efforts to suppress my response. Long, agonizing moments later he turns to pick up the clit clip, still perched beside my navel. Despite my concerns about an uncontrolled orgasm, my eyes are drawn back to the mirror. I watch, holding my breath as Dan tugs my clit, his actions firm and deft. He slips the small metal gadget over it. The arms close around the swollen bud trapping the blood there and holding it stiff and proud. He releases the clip to allow the beads to dangle tantalizingly on each side of my entrance before he turns to look at me.

"Well done. Do you like your new bling?"

"I do, Sir." I wriggle, causing the beads to swing and glitter. The sensation on my clit is indescribable. Certainly not painful, though I can feel the pressure. My clit is quivering, aching to be touched. I need Dan to do it. Or release my hands so I can do it myself.

"Please, it feels, I mean, would you…"

"Who are you talking to, Summer?"

"You, Sir. I'm sorry."

"I warned you of the consequences if you forgot yourself again. I won't tolerate disrespect."

"I meant no disrespect, Sir. It's just, I'm so..." My voice trails away as I run out of words to describe my predicament.

"So fucking horny you can't think straight." I should have known Dan would be able to help.

"That sounds about right, Sir."

"Little slut. You're lucky I'm such an easy-going Dom or I'd be spanking you right now."

"Please, could you do that later, Sir? Right now I want you to lick my clit."

Dan's eyebrow quirks, but he's smiling. As long as I call him Sir it seems I can talk as dirty as I like, be as demanding as I like.

"Say please, my slut."

"Please, Sir." My eyes are screwed up tight now, my clit and pussy throbbing as my desperation mounts. "Please. Please. Please."

"I almost faint with relief as he shifts on the bed, positioning himself between my legs. His hands on my inner thighs, he leans in to flick the tip of my clit with his tongue. "Like this, slut?"

"More, Sir. Harder, please."

He licks me with the flat of his tongue, causing the beads to tickle my inner lips as the clip shifts slightly.

"Oh, God. God, God, God," I mutter, throwing my head back as the familiar clench of orgasm starts low in my pussy and quickly grips me.

"Not God. Just Sir will do nicely."

"Sir. Sir. Sir. I need to come."

"Do it then." Then there are no more words. He dips his head again to take my clit between his teeth, flicking it sharply with his tongue before sucking gently.

I forget to breathe. All extraneous bodily functions are suspended as my orgasm seizes me and grabs hold hard. My pussy is spasming, and I could weep with gratitude when he plunges three slick fingers inside me to rub my G-spot. It's perfect. Every detail, every sensation exactly right, just what I want, what I need. I thrust my hips upwards, seeking more pressure, more friction, more of everything. Dan delivers, thrusting his fingers in and out fast and sucking on my clit until my orgasm peaks, then recedes. The warm afterglow is washing sweetly along my veins as he raises his head to drop a kiss on my stomach.

"Better now?"

I nod, unable to form words quite yet.

"Time to remove these."

I flinch as he flicks my right nipple, and realize I'd almost forgotten about the tight clamps gripping my hard buds. Almost, not quite.

"I can take the clamps off quickly, which hurts a lot but is soon over with. Or slowly, which is less painful, but lasts longer. Any preference?"

"No, Sir. You do what you think is best."

"Wise girl. I'll be quick then. Hold still."

Despite my best intentions, I squeal as the first clamp comes off and the blood supply is suddenly restored. Expecting this and ready for me, Dan's palm is across my mouth, not hard, but enough to muffle the sound.

"Rosie's asleep. We don't want to scare anyone, do we? Okay now?"

I nod, and he lifts his hand away.

"Next one?"

"Yes. Please, just do it, Sir."

Moments later his hand covers my mouth again as I can't restrain my scream. This is worse, much worse than the pressure he exerted as he applied the clamps, but it is mercifully swift. Dan tosses both nipple clamps onto the bedside table before applying his clever hands to my breasts, massaging both to draw the blood flow back and relieve the pain. It feels heavenly. I arch happily under his touch.

"You love this, don't you, my sweet slut."

"I do, Sir." No point in being coy at this stage in proceedings. Not at any stage, really. Here goes... "I'd love it even more if you'd fuck me, Sir."

"Great minds think alike, little sub. Roll over."

Or fools seldom differ, but who am I to argue?

"What about the other thing?"

"Other thing? Are you by some chance referring to my beautiful gold clit clip, the clit clip I bought especially for you and which is even now adorning your exquisitely hot and wet little tush? Would it be *that* thing you mean?"

"It would, Sir. Gold?"

"Yes, gold, you mercenary girl. And since you've asked, I want you to keep my gift on for a bit longer. Be careful you don't dislodge it when you move. Maybe you should close your legs."

"Makes a change, I suppose." I'm muttering to myself as I roll onto my side, then gingerly try to rearrange my body as instructed. I'm aching, and everything's awkward without the use of my hands. And while not uncomfortable exactly, I'm acutely conscious of the clip gripping my clit and the little dangling beads brushing against my delicate lips.

"Did you say something, slut?"

"No, Sir." My words are muffled as my cheek rests on the pillow. I'm unable to raise myself up onto all fours with my hands tied. He clearly has no intention of releasing me just yet, though he does test the restraints.

"Still comfortable?"

"Not really, Sir. My shoulders ache."

"Pity. Still, I'll make it worth your while. Arse in the air please."

I comply without making any comment, my weight tilted forward onto my shoulders. Dan grabs a couple of pillows and shoves them under my stomach. It makes no real difference to my comfort but ensures I won't be lowering my bum any time soon.

"I intend to fuck your arse. Will you scream, do you think?"

"I hope not, Sir."

"If you think you might scream, I want to know now and I'll gag you. I do *not* want you waking up the whole bloody house."

Well maybe you shouldn't make me scream so loud then...

"I think the gag, Sir." I'd hoped to avoid this. The prospect of a gag scares me. What if I need to safe word? What if I can't breathe? I voice my fears.

"You'll be fine. I'll check with you regularly." Dan sounds relaxed and certain of himself and his ability to take care of me.

He's given me no cause yet to doubt that and his confidence is reassuring. Maybe. A little. He continues, "And with the gag you'll be able to relax, you won't have to concentrate on keeping quiet. Open your mouth please."

Obedient submissive that I've become, despite my reluctance I part my lips and he pushes a scarf between my teeth. There's a knot in the middle, and this rests on my tongue, effectively silencing me. It doesn't restrict my breathing, but I hate it. I turn to bury my face in the pillow beneath me.

"Face the side please. I want to be able to see how you're doing."

I do as I'm told, feeling distinctly miserable. This is awful. I just want it to be over. Dan lifts my hair from my face.

"Tears, love?"

I can't answer, can't apologize, can't attempt to explain. And I suspect that crying while gagged will not end well. Running on sheer willpower now I suppress my aversion and bring my breathing under control.

"Good girl. Now the fun starts. Plenty of lube, I think."

And he's right. Incredibly, despite my hatred for the gag, the fun does indeed start the moment he inserts a lubricated fingertip into my anus. The muscle reacts immediately, slackening to allow entry. He pushes and his finger slides inside. He swirls it around, spreading the lube and loosening my entrance. I groan against the gag, the sound absorbed and deadened by the fabric. As if rewarding me for my cooperative response Dan reaches around me with his other hand to rub my engorged clit. The beads swing, brushing and tickling, and my clit stands to attention as he strums gently. It feels quite, quite wonderful.

He slides two fingers into my arse, twisting and scissoring to open my entrance. A third joins them, and he thrusts slowly to ensure my readiness. The finger on my clit combined with the lubing brings me rushing back to the brink of orgasm, and he's right about the liberating effect of the gag. I'm not able to tell him my release is close, but he knows anyway and slows his thrusting.

"Ready now, I think. Are you okay?"

I nod, and I mean it. I *am* okay.

He withdraws his fingers, and I turn my head to watch him as he unfastens his jeans. At first I assume he's just going to free his cock and fuck me fully dressed, but he doesn't do that. He undresses completely, taking his time and allowing me to look my fill. Despite his leisurely approach it is only a couple of minutes later when he extracts a condom from the bedside drawer and rips the foil. Sheathing himself swiftly he positions himself behind me. He inserts two fingers again, just to make sure, then the head of his thick cock is at my entrance.

"Slowly at first. I'll take good care of you, girl."

I close my eyes, settling in. I know he will look after me, I'm safe.

He eases his cock into my arse, inch by slow inch, his fingers caressing the delicate skin around my anus as he penetrates me. I feel cared for, adored. Loved even. Totally helpless, vulnerable, submissive. I surrender completely as his cock finally slides home. And I know, in that moment of intimate, sensual connection, I'm in love with Dan Riche.

I'm close to orgasm, very close, and I start to come almost as soon as he enters me fully. Dan doesn't seem to mind, heightens my response by flicking my clit again and murmuring encouragement. My pussy clenches on emptiness, but the fullness in my arse more than makes up for that. It feels wicked. The sensation is decadent and delightfully sinful, the hated gag just adding to the spice now. This orgasm is powerful, the intensity seemingly magnified by all the whistles and bells. He knows just how to play me, just what to do to coax and drag every shred of response from me. He seems to shoot past all my defenses, tossing my fears and anxieties and hang-ups aside. He sets me free.

And I feel free, supremely and brilliantly liberated as the waves of my orgasm cascade through my body.

I'm clenching, shuddering in release, all the while silenced by the gag when I would have screamed my joy in this moment. Dan thrusts long and slow and deep, his strokes even as my body stretches to accept and glory in this intrusion. As the climax passes I let my weight rest entirely on the pillows under me. I feel light-headed, boneless, more than a little stunned at the intensity of the feeling.

Dan reaches down to hook his hands under my shoulders and pulls me up against his chest. Still sunk deep inside me, he eases me up to straddle his knees, holding me in place with one arm across my chest while he arranges my legs on either side of his. I'm opened, available, totally his to touch, to use, to fuck. He turns on the bed, carrying me with him, to face the floor-length mirror fastened to one wall. My eyes are drawn to the tableau, the scarf he's used to gag me a shock of crimson across my face. My nipples are still swollen and erect, almost as bright red as the gag, and I can clearly see the beads dangling from my clit. When I'm waxed, the view will be even more alluring.

"You're so beautiful, Summer. Everywhere. Inside and out. And so courageous you take my breath away. What can I do for you now, I wonder?"

Who knows? Surely there's nothing left.

Wrong!

Two fingers plunging into my pussy quickly rekindle my interest. With his customary unerring accuracy Dan finds and caresses my G-spot. I can't manage to keep my eyes open as the sensation builds and grasps me once more. I'd thought I was spent, nothing left. I was wrong. I rest my head against his shoulder, unable to stop myself gyrating and writhing on his cock. Dan allows it, permits me to increase the friction enough to climax again, less powerfully this time but all the sweeter for the intimacy of our connection. This is for me, all for me. Dan is demanding, totally dominant, sometimes intimidating. But he's generous too, gentle when he needs to be, and completely focused on my pleasure right now.

I drink it in, savor his gift as my release overwhelms me again, before sliding away like a liquid caress. I'm warm, soft and pliable, his to fuck as he likes, my surrender total.

Dan lowers me back until my shoulders are resting on the bed again, my knees still bent and my bum still lifted for his pleasure. And now it's his turn. He withdraws until only the head of his cock is still inside me before thrusting deep again. This time he plunges hard and fast, but I'm so ready for him it doesn't hurt me. He drives his cock in and out of my arse easily, each stroke filling me delightfully. I squeeze around him as his increasingly fevered moans tell me he's close. With a shout of "holy fuck" he's there. His final thrust is hard and sharp, then he holds still deep inside as his semen spurts to fill the condom. It occurs to me that he's not been exactly silent himself, but on reflection I have no complaints.

* * * *

"Am I forgiven? For the gag?"

I'm lying across Dan's chest, his arms around me as we snuggle together in his bed. The crimson scarf is on the floor, the clit clip safely deposited in a small tray on the bedside table. Nine karat gold. Wow!

"Ask me in the morning. I'm too tired to think right now."

"I'm asking you now. You can start by telling me you're okay. I want to know."

"Yes, I'm okay. Very okay." I try to burrow deeper into his chest.

"And the gag? How do you feel about that?"

It seems I'm not going to sleep any time soon. Dan's tone has developed that firm edge I recognize, that timbre that tells me I *will* be answering his questions. And I'll be giving him his answers now, no matter how sleepy I am. I take a moment or two to rake my scattered thoughts and impressions into something resembling coherence.

"I hated it at first. But when we got started, I sort of forgot it was there."

"Why did you hate it?"

"Mostly because it scared me. I was worried I wouldn't be able to breathe."

"I was watching you the whole time, making sure you were safe. I'll never put you in danger, or harm you. But I will scare you. Again and again. Are you still up for that?" His palm circles my back, between my shoulder blades. His touch is soothing despite his hardening tone.

"I know you won't harm me. I do, really..."

"Don't hedge, Summer. Answer my question." The palm ceases its calming caress as he lifts his hand to tangle in my hair.

He gently tilts my head back so I'm looking up at him. His eyes are dark, intense and serious. And he's waiting for my answer.

"Yes, I am up for it. Sir." My voice is soft, little more than a whisper.

He smiles at me, his expression softening, reassuring me despite the threat implied in his words.

"I'm glad. I appreciate that you're inexperienced, but you're learning fast and I intend to push you hard. Even harder than I have up to now. And the best orgasms come after you've been scared. Don't you agree?

Well, I can't really argue with that. "I do, Sir, but the gag was still difficult to accept."

He nods slightly, quirking one eyebrow. "You did accept it, though. Eventually."

"You have a way of distracting me. And you were right about the screaming thing. I didn't have to concentrate on being quiet. That was good."

His grin widens as he leans down to kiss my forehead. "Mmm, you're not bad yourself. So would you let me gag you again?"

"Yes, of course. Anything." I'm surprised he's even asking, especially as I've just more or less given him carte blanche to do whatever he likes to me. He normally just produces whatever he intends to use and orders me to assume the required position.

"I'll remind you of that next time you get the wobbles." He kisses my hair, and the conversation seems to be over.

He's disturbed me now though. I'm thoroughly awake and I have another question.

"When do you leave? Tomorrow I mean."

"Not early. I'll see you off to Leeds, then I'll be away."

"I'll miss you." I bury my nose against his shoulder, trying to imagine Black Combe without Dan here.

"I'll miss you too. But I'll be back soon. Ten days at the most I should think. And you'll be busy. New job and all that."

But will he be? I need to ask him something else. For my own peace of mind, I need to know.

"When you're at home again, will you go to the club do you think?"

He stiffens. I feel the shift in his muscles, the slight tightening of his arms around my back. Maybe I shouldn't have asked, but I'm entitled to know. Surely. Especially now.

He doesn't reply immediately, but I know he heard me and I don't repeat my question.

"No, I won't be going to the club." At last, he speaks.

Thank God! "Good. I mean, I won't be… I won't… Well, I won't either."

"Somehow I'd never imagined you would." He leans down to drop another kiss on my hair.

"Well, right. But I wanted you to know. And I wondered, well…" This is difficult to put into words.

"I think I know what you wondered, what's behind all this. You want to know if this, you and me, is an exclusive arrangement. Am I right?" As usual, Dan helps me out.

He doesn't sound aggrieved, doesn't seem to have taken my question amiss. I'm squirming though. I've never been especially at ease around men, well, not before now. Even James was always something of a mystery to me, more a means to an end I now see. But Dan's different. Dan is more, so much more. I love him, so it's simple really. And I need to know.

"Yes, Sir. That's right."

"Well, we are. At least, as far as I'm concerned we are. I don't object, in principle, to sharing subs as long as everyone's happy with the arrangement. But I've no intention of sharing you."

Thank God for that too. "I don't share either." No harm in trying for a little assertiveness, even now.

"Fair enough. We're agreed then?"

Wow! Easy as that. "Yes. Thank you, Sir."

"You're welcome. And, thank *you*, Summer, for raising the issue. I get the impression it wasn't easy."

"No, Sir. I was afraid you'd think I was being pushy. Too demanding. Possessive."

"You're none of those things, Summer. And just in case you have any remaining doubts about this, never be afraid to ask me anything. I may not choose to answer every time, but you are entitled to ask your questions. Always. I'm a Dom, but that doesn't make me aloof or an arrogant bastard. Well, not that arrogant anyway. I won't be offended, I'm not moody, and I won't punish you just for being curious or unsure. Talk to me, whenever you need to. Say whatever you need to say."

I hesitate for a few moments, taking in what he's telling me. I have a strong sense of our relationship solidifying around me, around us. A deal has been struck, promises exchanged. At last, I respond. "I see. Thank you, Sir.

"I think you do. I'm glad. Again, you're welcome. So, sleep now, little sub?"

"Mmm." I snuggle in, one seriously happy and well-fucked submissive. Ten days isn't really so long.

Chapter Eleven

Dan wakes first, but instead of seducing me into another bout of frenzied fucking, which would after all have been so easy, he takes pity on my soreness and settles for licking my clit until I come. Then he does it again, just for good measure, before ambling off downstairs in just his jeans to rustle up coffee and breakfast. He returns with two steaming mugs and a plate of toasted crumpets, dripping with butter. We eat in companionable silence, listening to the house waking up around us. Rapid footsteps on the landing outside signal that Rosie is up and about and hurtling downstairs to be fed. The lighter tread a couple of minutes later is Eva, probably carrying baby Isabella. Dan said that Nathan and Grace were already down in the kitchen when he launched his raid. So that just leaves us languishing in bed.

I love the quiet intimacy of this breakfast in bed together, the feeling that I'm cared about, and safe. My future seems secure, and I'm happy. Genuinely happy, untroubled. All I need to do now, to complete my sense of well-being, is to somehow get my sisters to come and live here with me. I really have no idea how my mother will react to that proposal. I suppose I'll have to phone her, go and talk to her even. I don't relish that prospect, and I just know that this could get ugly. I'm determined to have my way, though, and I'll fight as dirty as I have to.

But first things first. I need to say my goodbyes to Dan, then get Freya's car to her, then choose myself a bed. I have my instructions on that, and a four-poster it will be.

It's mid-morning before Eva and I leave for Leeds. I manage not to weep all over Dan's lovely white T-shirt when he hugs me just before I scramble into the Vanquish. His whispered "Keep everything warm for me, little sub" sets my pussy off dampening again — he really does not play fair.

I mutter something along the lines of "I'll try", and "Please come back soon" before I scuttle into the driver's seat.

Dan leans on the side of the car, watching as I adjust the positioning of everything to suit my size. Eva's jolly little Mini emerges from the huge hanger-like garage a few moments later, to hum into line behind me.

We'll drive to Leeds in convoy, deposit the Vanquish with Freya, then continue on in the Mini. In the end Grace decided not to come with us. There's an open day on at Rosie's school and she's promised to be there. Nathan apparently intends to go too, so Rosie was almost dancing with excitement as Grace bundled her into her school uniform before driving her down into the village.

Dan taps twice on the car roof, signaling it's time to go. I lift my hand in a silent salute but that's not sufficient. He swirls his finger to indicate I should lower the window, and when I do he leans in to give me a long, deep kiss. He slides his tongue between my lips, seeking, tasting, marking me as his. At last he breaks the kiss, lifting his lips from mine just enough to be able to murmur his farewell. "Just to remind you what you have to look forward to when I get back. Choose our bed wisely, little sub."

"Yes, Sir. Please come back soon."

"As soon as I can. I promise. Drive carefully." With a final smile, and a wink which is more than a little suggestive he stands back.

Heavy hearted I pull away, insisting to myself that the next week and a half will simply fly by. It has to. As I pass the house I wave to Nathan who's come out onto his front step to see us off, baby Isabella in his arms. I glance in the mirror to see Eva blowing kisses to him from her car as she follows me along the gravel. Dan is striding back to join him, and the two of them wait on the step until we round the corner taking us out of sight.

Ten whole days before I see him again. Shit. But still, my stomach does a delightful little flip at the prospect of his return. I hug myself, giggling like the teenager I never quite dared to be.

* * * *

We pull into the underground parking area serving Nathan's exclusive apartment building in Leeds' Clarence Dock, and Eva texts Freya to check if it's okay to go up. We wouldn't want our unannounced arrival to be awkward, after all. A few seconds pass, then Eva's phone pings as the text is returned. She reads, frowning, then passes the phone to me.

Yes, come up. Just me here. Nick went back to Cartmel.

"Well, so much for a make-up spanking. I wonder what all this is about." Eva pockets the phone and strides out for the lift. I hurry after her, every bit as curious.

Eva lets us into the apartment with her key card, and we find a red-eyed Freya huddled on the sofa. She looks awful, haggard even. From the look of her I'd be prepared to bet she got no sleep last night, but whether her grief is primarily for her beloved horse, or the relationship she struggled so hard for and which now seems to lie in tatters I'm not sure. I sit next to her, open my arms and she crawls into my embrace, hugging me as if she's drowning. Neither Eva nor I ask her any questions initially. There would be no point. Her heaving, silent sobs are racking her small, curvy form. I just hold her, patting her back uselessly while Eva busies herself with the kettle.

At last, though, a pot of tea steaming on the low table in front of the sofa, I manage to prise Freya out of my arms.

"So, Cartmel? What the fuck is he doing in Cartmel?" Eva starts the interrogation

I might have phrased it differently, but that does just about capture the essence. Eva's not known for her powers of tact and diplomacy, and at this moment I'm glad of it. We both wait expectantly.

"He was angry. Too angry, he said, to deal with me yet. So he went."

"Yet? Did you say yet?" I'm struggling to get to grips with all this, but there does seem to be a gleam of hope in there somewhere. Well hidden, mind you.

Freya nods, her misery completely apparent.

"So he's coming back?" This from Eva.

She is answered by another feeble nod from Freya.

"When?" Me again.

Freya shrugs, so I press her harder. "What? Don't you know?"

She shakes her head. "He told me to wait here, or go back to Kendal if I want to. He'll be in touch."

"What, sort of don't call me, I'll call you?"

I can tell Eva doesn't think much of this waiting game, and Freya looks totally unraveled by the whole thing. I can sort of understand Nick's logic, though, and despite my friend's obvious distress I appreciate his restraint. Having been on the receiving end of physical discipline at Dan's hands a couple of times now, I can completely sympathize with his decision. If I'm following this correctly, Nick has opted to delay punishing Freya until he's no longer angry with her. This is for her safety, her protection.

"I know what you're thinking, but he will be back. He promised." Despite her grief, Freya is glaring at Eva, her expression fierce.

"Sorry, I know. I know that. He loves you. But still, couldn't he have stayed to see you through all this with the horse?" Eva hands Freya a cup of tea.

She takes it and sips delicately so we have to wait for her response to Eva's latest point. I know all Freya's tricks for delaying when she's collecting her thoughts so I resist relieving her of her cup. For now at least. My patience pays off as she sets the teacup down and resumes her explanation.

"Yes, he does. And he helped me all he could with Queenie. I really don't know what I'd have done yesterday without him. And Dan." She looks to the door and back to us. "Where *is* Dan?"

"He had to go back to Cumbria. He has to work. He'll be back in a week or so."

Freya nods. "I see. Right. So, are you and Dan…?

Now it's my turn to nod. "We are. And I'll tell you all about that, but not right now. Right now we want to know how you are, what Nick intends to do, when he intends to do it, and how's your horse?"

Freya heaves a great sigh before starting on her reply. Her hands are light and nimble as she frames her signing, "I'm fine. Miserable, lonely, but fine. I'm glad to see you two—thank you for coming. I don't know what Nick intends to do, but I know it'll hurt. It'll be worth it, though, because afterwards he'll forgive me. I know he will, and we'll be okay again. Queenie seems comfortable, and the vets at the hospital seem optimistic but I'm going back there later this afternoon. Did you bring my car, by the way?"

"Yes, it's in the underground parking bay." I fish the keys from my jacket pocket and place them on the coffee table. "We're going furniture shopping. I'm moving into a flat above the garage at Black Combe. Accommodation goes with the job you got for me. Did I thank you for that. By the way?"

Freya's disgusted expression indicates just what she thinks of the need for thanks, so I continue, "It needs furnishing, so we're headed to Ikea after this. Want to come?"

"I'd love to, but I can't. I want to go to the veterinary hospital to see how Queenie's doing, and Nick told me to stay here."

"What, you're not allowed to go out? We'll be back in time for you to visit your horse."

"He didn't say I wasn't to go anywhere, and maybe he never intended it. But I'm not risking it. Apart from visiting Queenie, or essentials like shopping for food, I'm staying here. As instructed."

Eva and I both know when to admit defeat. It's clear Freya's in no mood for Ikea today. I doubt if Nick ever truly meant her to be confined to the apartment, but I suppose she's doing what she thinks is right. And while on that subject...

"Freya, what *was* all that about? I don't understand— Why didn't you tell Nick about the money?"

She looks from me to Eva and back again, then picks up her cup. Delaying tactics again. I'm ready to wait her out. Eva seems to be going nowhere either. We both sip our tea, expectant, patient, determined to get to the bottom of this.

"I couldn't. I meant to, all along I meant to, but I didn't, and it just got harder and harder as time went by."

Eva and I exchange a look which indicates that neither of us is any closer to enlightenment. Freya catches it, and seems to take umbrage. "Oh, right, and neither of you ever had a secret then? Something private that you didn't want to share?"

Ah, right. But even so, being minted is hardly on a par with my dirty little secret that I haven't even shared with Freya let alone Dan. I sneak a glance at Eva, who is looking thoughtful. She nods slowly, seemingly closer to understanding Freya's point of view than I am.

"So, okay then, I can understand that things sort of escalated. But why start the deception in the first place. Did you think he was only interested in you because you're rich?"

"No! Never. Quite the opposite in fact. Summer knows that. I couldn't get him to accept money when I offered it to him. Nick was never motivated by greed. I knew that from the beginning." Freya's vehement defense of Nick's moral fiber is encouraging on one level, but does nothing to dispel our utter confusion.

"So…?" Eva is perplexed, but still trying. Maybe this is her innate need to understand, to explain, all traits of the rigorous academic which she is.

For myself, I'm starting to become resigned to living with the messy uncertainty. It's clear that Freya doesn't know herself why she let the situation get so out of hand.

"I'm sorry. I messed up. Totally screwed things up. Is Nathan very angry? About the board meeting I mean?"

Eva looks surprised. "No, I don't think so. He was caught on the back-foot and he doesn't usually take too kindly to that. But his main concern was for you. Still is."

Freya stiffens her posture, her expression serious now. I've seen that look before. She means business.

"Please would you tell him that I *will* be making that investment. Max will be in touch regarding the details. Whatever happens with Nick, I know he won't interfere with that. He won't want to, although I'm determined to include him if I can. We'll see how that goes."

"Okay, I'll pass that on. Are you sure you won't come to Ikea with us. We're shopping for four-poster beds."

Freya smiles at that, the first proper sign that the old Freya might be re-emerging from under her cocoon of abject misery. "Four-posters? Whose idea was that then?"

"Dan's," Eva puts in helpfully. "And Nathan seems to think we need one too. Summer's asked Dan to get some red silk rope."

Freya just lifts one eyebrow as she reaches for the teapot to pour us all a top-up. I guess Ikea will have to wait for half an hour or so while I discuss the relative merits of silk rope or leather straps with these my friends who are so much more experienced in these matters.

* * * *

In fact it's another ninety minutes before we all three make our way back down to the underground car park—Freya on her way to the hospital to check on Queenie's progress, and Eva and myself en route to some sprawling retail park on the Leeds ring road. We have a group hug beside Freya's car, then she slips into her driver's seat and starts the engine. Eva and I watch her purr out of the car park. I'm conscious that the next few days or weeks will not be easy, but at the same time I'm confident that eventually this will all be behind her. I just hope Nick's temper doesn't take too long to cool. The waiting is the hardest part.

The shopping expedition passes in something of a blur. Eva has the company credit card, and makes purchase after purchase for my new home. I keep trying to stop her, convinced I really don't need so much stuff.

"It's a big flat, you'll need beds for your sisters, enough chairs. Cupboards. You never have enough storage space. What about your shoes?"

I can safely say my shoes would fit in, well, in a shoebox I suppose. I don't have a lot of stuff of my own, just the contents of my holdall tucked under Dan's bed, and a few items still at Freya's apartment. A modest chest of drawers and a wardrobe would be ample. Eva has other ideas, though, and by the end of the afternoon what seems to me to be a lorry-load of gear is scheduled for delivery over the coming few days.

We drew a blank on four-posters, though. Perhaps there's not much call for such things among Ikea's normal clientele. The salesman looked rather nonplussed when we enquired, explaining patiently that the modern customer tended to favor divans, sled beds, something more contemporary. He pointed out the merits of under-bed storage, and of course I can see he has a point. We'll need somewhere to store Dan's whips. Even so, we really did have our hearts set on a four-poster. Still, I'm pragmatic, ready to settle for something nice from their king-size range.

Not so Eva. There's to be no settling for a common-or-garden divan for her, even if it does come with drawers underneath. She has her instructions, and it seems Nathan's commands are not to be thwarted just because Ikea wants to cater to the mass market. "Please can you arrange for delivery of the stuff we've ordered so far? We'll need to think about the bed."

"Of course. Can I take some details?" We spend the next twenty minutes filling in forms, getting our credit card payment authorized, our purchases duly completed, and delivery details finalized. And we're still missing two four-poster beds.

Eva seems unconcerned. "Right, I've worked up an appetite. They do a wonderful Swedish meatballs dish here. Let's hit the café, order some food, and sort out our four-posters."

I can't imagine we'll find what we're looking for on the menu in the Ikea restaurant, but my feet ache and the meatballs sound interesting. I don't take a lot of persuading. Eva orders meatballs and mash for two, then digs in her bag for her iPad. She fires it up and starts Googling four-poster beds.

Less than ten minutes later, we've found a specialist supplier in Devon who makes beds to order and can deliver anywhere in the UK. There's an online ordering system, but Eva insists on phoning them up to find out how quickly they could process an order from us. Very quickly indeed, it seems. Perhaps trade is less brisk than they would like. In any case, the bed I fancy, a rather solid but still graciously proportioned piece called the Hanover, could it seems, be erected in my bedroom within five days.

"Is that the one you want?" Eva shoves the iPad back under my nose for a last, decisive look.

I shake my head in disbelief. "Shit, Eva. It costs twelve hundred quid. We could get one of those with drawers for under two hundred. And two free bedside lights thrown in."

"Dan doesn't want drawers. Or lights. He wants posts to tie you to, and cross bars to hang you from. Are we going to disappoint him?"

Absolutely not. But still — twelve hundred pounds... I shake my head uncertainly. Eva harbors no such misgivings.

"Right, this one it is then." She returns her attention to the salesperson on the end of the phone, who is no doubt extremely interested in her remarks regarding our particular requirements in a bed. "We'll take the Hanover. In dark oak I think. And I also want a Tudor, in walnut. Yes, that's right, two beds please. Yes, both need to be king size. Next Thursday will be fine. The delivery men *will* assemble them for us, won't they?"

She completes the deal, and is just hanging up as our meatballs arrive. A good day's work, it seems. Well, Eva's pleased with herself, and I suppose I've no complaints. And neither Dan nor Nathan will find any cause to grumble at our choice.

Chapter Twelve

The next week flew past in a blur. I miss Dan, I think. When I remember to. Most of the time I'm frantically busy. Nathan spent a fair bit of time with me in the first couple of days, explaining to me the various projects that he and Tom have in hand. He provided me with a long list of their key contacts — solicitors, accountants, surveyors, bankers, research teams, marketing, PR, and instructed me to make myself known to them in my new capacity as Projects Manager with Darke Associates. He had a meeting with the company lawyers on my second day at work and insisted I accompany him. He also introduced me to the firm of accountants who handle our business, with instructions I be added as a signatory to the current account.

I've spent hours and hours reading through files and familiarizing myself with the day-to-day workings of the company. I'm to concentrate on the music festival, primarily because that's such a big project, a lot of money is tied up in it and it's very high profile. The local community has mixed feelings. Local traders naturally welcome the influx of visitors who will all want feeding, accommodating, entertaining, but there will no doubt be complaints about traffic, noise, litter. It all needs managing carefully if the parish council are to remain supportive. Nathan insists that we need to keep the locals on side.

"We live in this community. These are the parents of Rosie's school friends, and Isabella's too in a couple of years' time. It's bad enough that Tom and I can't get served in the local pub because of the wind farm proposal, I don't want Rosie banned from the Brownies."

Excellent public spirited sentiment. I make a note to suggest offering a reduced price entry ticket for local residents to come to the festival. I've been doing my research about wind farms too, and I've discovered that there would need to be a community levy, a percentage of the revenue to be invested in local projects to help offset the nuisance of it all. The sooner we start talking to the parish council about how that should be spent the better, I reckon.

Meanwhile the wind farm planning application needs to be prepared and submitted. We are using a firm of planning specialists, but they need instructing and chasing to maintain the momentum, especially now that the finance aspect seems to be resolved. Max Furrowes, Freya's personal banking consultant and fund manager, has been in touch, confirming his client's interest in investing in the scheme, so I've been liaising with the legal advisers to get the contracts drawn up.

Ashley's pet scheme of establishing Greystones as a wedding and events venue is also a key priority, and that will be starting from scratch. She only mentioned weddings and parties when we spoke before she headed off on her honeymoon, but I'm wondering about training events and conferences too. I've started to look into the public liability implications, checking out insurances and so on. By the time Ashley gets back I'd like to be able to show her some detailed and costed proposals, and perhaps a timescale for getting the project started.

Maybe I'm trying too hard, and I probably can't maintain this pace for very long, but I really do want my new employers to be impressed. I feel this job just sort of fell into my lap at exactly the time I needed it, and I don't want anyone to regret employing me. I'm determined to give Darke Associates their money's worth.

And on the plus side, as a result of this frenzy of industrious activity, I've had almost no time to brood over Dan Riche. Almost no time at all to count down the days until he can be back. He didn't say exactly what day he'd return in any case, but it shouldn't be long now. Not that I'm fretting. Not much.

Yeah, right.

The day of the bed delivery is momentous. I'm watching from the office window as the Classic Beds' van lumbers up our drive and circles the gravel forecourt before drawing to a halt beside Nathan's garage. I spot them arriving from my desk in the office and rush out to direct them up to the flat. Grace joins me, and between us we supervise the unloading and humping up the stairs of my beautiful four-poster. It's come in lots of separate pieces, thank goodness, and the delivery men seem quite unfazed by the stairs. I suppose they usually do find themselves manhandling these things up at least one flight. They pile all the bits in the middle of my freshly carpeted bedroom floor, and set to assembling them. An hour later, all is in place, the solid posts dominating my spacious room, the lofty cross pieces crying out for curtains. And maybe the odd hook or metal loop. I think we may be adding those later. I doubt they come as standard.

The poor delivery crew are looking slightly jaded as they head off across the courtyard toward the main house to start all over again under Eva's eagle-eyed supervision.

Grace disappears as the van crunches off back across the gravel, only to re-emerge up the stairs ten minutes later carrying a pile of curtains. She drops everything on top of the new mattress and tells me to get started trying to figure out how to hang the drapery around the bed. On closer inspection I note that the bed hangings match the curtains at my bedroom window, a delicate pattern of light greys and lilac. It's feminine, but not oppressively so.

Grace disappears again, but is back after a few minutes carrying my bed linen. The sheets and pillow cases are in a soft lilac shade to tone perfectly with the curtains, and the duvet cover is a beautiful pearl gray. The whole lot will lot gorgeous when the bed's made up.

Hanging the drapery from the posts is not a simple affair. That project takes us a whole hour to accomplish as neither me nor Grace have ever dressed a four-poster bed before, but we figure it out between us. When we eventually get the sheets fitted, the duvet wrestled into its cover, and the whole lot prettily laid out, it does look quite stunning. Grace will be a dab hand by the time she gets stuck in to Eva and Nathan's bed.

"Oh yes, I was right about this. A four-poster is perfect for in here." Grace stands back to admire her creation,

I can't help agreeing with her, though I suspect my approval owes little to the finer points of soft furnishing

* * * *

It's been nine days. He'll be back tomorrow. Probably. Dan didn't promise, he wasn't specific, but he said ten days and that takes us to tomorrow.

I've moved into my flat now. Yesterday I slept here for the first time. My kitchen is fully installed, my fridge well stocked from the Black Combe larder. Grace does all the shopping, for everyone. A mountain of groceries is delivered by a Tesco van which trundles up here about once a month. Grace orders enough to feed a Third World country and stores it in the massive walk-in fridge at Black Combe. Tom and Ashley help themselves to whatever they need, and leave a hundred quid or so on the kitchen table. This system apparently evolved when Tom lived on his own at Greystones and Grace was convinced he couldn't look after himself. I doubt he was ever that helpless, but it's suited everyone to just carry on with it, even though Tom's no longer living alone. I daresay we get the economies of bulk buying, and Grace thinks it would be easiest if I just join in too. I have to admit the system has its attractions. I'm not that fond of supermarket shopping, and I'm not much of a cook really. Freya tended to deal with all that side of things when we were in Kendal, and when I'm by myself I just sort of muddle through.

Obviously I'll need to buck up my ideas once Lucy and Maisie move in. I can't put off that conversation with my mother for much longer.

It's just after six in the evening when I close down my laptop in the office. I stop off in the kitchen for a cup of tea and a chat with Grace before ambling across the gravel to my own flat. Grace invites me to eat at Black Combe this evening. I've taken all my evening meals with Grace, Eva and Nathan since I arrived but this time I decline. It's kind of her, and I don't suppose anyone would really mind if I was there all the time. Now that I'm over my initial intimidation at the size of the house, and got to know its occupants, I've come to realize that Black Combe is a busy, friendly place, full of chatter and laughter. But I have my own flat, and I want to spend my evening here. I'm putting down roots.

I kick my shoes off inside the door and head for the shower. It's been a hard day, enjoyable, demanding, satisfying and utterly exhausting. But I made a lot of progress and I'm quietly pleased with myself. I'm getting established as the face of Darke Associates— people ask for me on the phone, send me emails. I'm humming as I dump my clothes in the linen basket, thinking I might fill the automatic washer later. I turn on the jets and I step in, sighing as the hot water cascades over me. The strains of a day spent laboring over a hot laptop are rinsed away with the streaming water. I lean my forehead against the tiles, the chilly surface warming under the hot spray, and reach for the shampoo.

"Let me."

"What!" I whirl, to find myself caught, pulled against a solid, naked male chest and soundly kissed.

Dan! How? Where? My head abandons the effort. I give up trying to process and simply accept that he's here. Naked with me in my shower. Kissing me.

A day early. *Oh. My God.*

About the Author

Until 2010, Ashe was a director of a regeneration company before deciding there had to be more to life and leaving to pursue a lifetime goal of self-employment.

Ashe has been an avid reader of women's fiction for many years—erotic, historical, contemporary, fantasy, romance—you name it, as long as it's written by women, for women. Now, at last in control of her own time and working from her home in rural West Yorkshire, she has been able to realise her dream of writing erotic romance herself.

She draws on settings and anecdotes from her previous and current experience to lend colour, detail and realism to her plots and characters, but her stories of love, challenge, resilience and compassion are the conjurings of her own imagination. She loves to craft strong, enigmatic men and bright, sassy women to give them a hard time—in every sense of the word.

When she's not writing, Ashe's time is divided between her role as resident taxi driver for her teenage daughter, and caring for a menagerie of dogs, cats, rabbits, tortoises and a hamster.

Ashe Barker loves to hear from readers. You can find her contact information, website details and author profile page at http://www.totallybound.com.

Totally Bound Publishing

Made in the USA
San Bernardino, CA
29 December 2017